THE MEDUSA PROJECT
THE THIEF

This book has been specially written and published for World Book Day 2010. World Book Day is a worldwide celebration of books and reading, with events held last year in countries as far apart as Afghanistan and Australia, Nigeria and Uruguay. For further information please see www.worldbookday.com

World Book Day in the UK and Ireland is made possible by generous sponsorship from National Book Tokens, participating publishers, authors and booksellers. Booksellers who accept the £1 World Book Day Token kindly agree to bear the full cost of redeeming it.

Also by Sophie McKenzie:

www.sophiemckenziebooks.com

SOPHIE McKENZIE

THE MEDUSA PROJECT
THE THIEF

SIMON AND SCHUSTER

For Sarah

This World Book Day book published in Great Britain by
Simon and Schuster UK Ltd/Hachette Children's Books, 2010

Cover illustration by Sam Hadley

Simon & Schuster UK Ltd, A CBS Company
1st Floor, 222 Gray's Inn Road, London WC1X 8HB

A CIP catalogue record for this book
is available from the British Library.

ISBN: 978-0-95628-778-6

www.simonandschuster.co.uk
www.sophiemckenziebooks.com
www.themedusaproject.co.uk

Fourteen years ago, scientist William Fox implanted four babies with the Medusa gene – a gene for psychic abilities. Now dead, his experiment left a legacy: four teenagers – Nico, Ketty, Ed and William's own daughter, Dylan – each of whom have developed their own distinct and special skill.

Brought together by government agent, Geri Paterson, the four make up the Medusa Project – a secret, government-funded, crime-fighting force.

Until recently, the Medusa teens lived under the protection of William's brother, Fergus Fox, at his North London boarding school – Fox Academy. However their existence has now become known to members of the criminal underworld, so they are being taken to a secluded training camp where their identities can be kept secret.

Nico: midnight

The news came when I was asleep in the back of the car. Ketty shook me awake to tell me.

'Nico,' she said. '*Nico.*'

In my dream she was kissing me . . .

'Nico.' Ketty shook my arm harder. '*Wake up.*'

Grumbling at being wrenched from my dream, I forced my eyes open.

'He knows where we're headed.' Ketty was right beside me in the car. Her eyes were wide, horrified, as she spoke.

'What?' I said, blinking properly awake. 'Who?'

'It's Foster.' James, one of the agents assigned to protect us, glanced over his shoulder from the front passenger seat. 'I've just had a message from HQ. Apparently he knows which private airport we're taking you to.'

I squeezed Ketty's hand. I wasn't too worried about Damian Foster. We'd fought him off before. We could do it again.

'It'll be all right, babe.'

Ketty nodded. She's cool, my girlfriend.

Unusual too – well, all four of us are. We're the Medusa Project. Each of us has a particular psychic gift. Mine's telekinesis; Ketty can see into the future.

Last night, Foster tried to kill us. We only just escaped. Our school got blown up too – which is why we were in a car, past midnight, driving away from our old life and heading for two months in some kind of training camp.

'According to our intelligence, Foster is on his way to the same private airport we're taking you to,' James said.

'How did he find out where we're going?' I asked.

'Must have been his spy in the security services,' Ketty said.

I glanced at our driver, Maria. She nodded, her mouth a grim line in the rear-view mirror.

Maria and James were our escorts for the journey to training camp. They'd been assigned to us by Geri Paterson – the woman in charge of the Medusa Project. We'd known Maria for a while. She'd given us regular defence and attack training for the past few weeks. James was a newer member of Geri's team. He'd been drugged and left unconscious for a few minutes by Foster's accomplice earlier tonight, but was fine now.

'So what happens now?' I asked.

'We change our route . . . take you to a different location for the night,' James explained.

'Where?' Ketty asked.

James and Maria exchanged looks.

'We're discussing it with Geri at the moment,' Maria said.

'Don't worry,' James added. 'It'll be somewhere Foster can't possibly find you.'

He sounded confident. A bit *over*confident, if you asked me. He was in his late twenties, I reckoned, with the look of a bloke trying too hard to be young – you know, leather jacket, over-gelled hair. Maria, on the other hand, was all skinny in jeans with long blonde hair and dangly earrings. Quite fit, actually, if you're into the Older Woman. Not that I am. I'm all about one girl.

My girl.

Ketty.

It's not so much that she's pretty, though she is . . . *very*. It's more . . . that she's got her own way of doing things, like being obsessed with running and tying her hair back with bits of string. Ketty doesn't care what other people think.

Beside me, she yawned. I checked the time. It was nearly one a.m.

'Have you had any sleep?' I whispered, putting my arm round her.

'Not yet.' She laid her head against my chest. Her curly brown hair tickled my chin. 'We'll be okay, won't we, Nico?'

'Course we will,' I said. 'James and Maria know what they're doing. It's just a detour.'

We sat in silence for a while.

'Close your eyes,' I whispered. 'You need to sleep.'

A few minutes later I felt Ketty's body sink down, heavy against mine. I sat as still as I could, so as not to wake her. Dylan and Ed were sleeping too. Dylan was sitting directly in front of me, her long red hair fanned out on either side of the seat. Ed was next to her. Light snores burbled out of his mouth. He and Dylan had both worked hard today too. Ed had read Foster's mind, which had made him puke, and Dylan had used her protective skills to keep us all safe.

I leaned forward and teleported Dylan's mp3 player off her lap and into my hands. I detached the headphones and spun the device in circles above my hand.

I wasn't sleepy myself any more. Was this what life was going to be like forever now? Either dealing with bad guys or running away from them?

'Why does Foster want *us*?' I asked, letting the mp3 player drop into my hand.

'Revenge, probably,' Maria said from the front.

James twisted round to look at me. 'Or else he wants to know more about what you can do.' He paused. 'That's quite an array of talents the four of you have.'

I shrugged, spinning the mp3 player into the air again. James watched, transfixed.

'Hey, what're you doing?' Dylan had woken up and was frowning at me through the gap in the seats. She reached towards the mp3 player. 'Give that back, jerkwad. That's mine.'

I rolled my eyes and sent the device tumbling through the air towards Dylan. She snatched at it, knocking Ed's shoulder. He woke with a start.

'Er . . . what's going on?' he said. His hair was all tufty and tousled, making him look even geekier than usual. 'Where are we?'

Maria explained quickly about Foster and our need to take a detour.

James's phone beeped. He picked it up. 'Message from Geri . . .' He paused, then turned to Maria. 'She's gone for it.'

'Gone for what?' I asked.

'Our new location for the night,' James explained. 'A house in Lymewich in Kent . . . near the coast. We're only about twenty minutes away.'

'An *ordinary* house?' I glanced at Dylan.

She frowned, picking up on my concerns straight away. 'Not a *safe* house?' she said.

Maria shrugged. 'We've been messaging on an encrypted line. HQ think you'll be as safe there as anywhere. The important thing is that Foster won't have any idea where you are.'

'We could go to a hotel, but Lymewich is close. It's actually my parents' place – a holiday home. The address isn't on any of my files,' James went on. 'It's a good choice.'

'Sure,' Dylan muttered, 'let's keep it in the family.'

'Will your parents be there?' Ed asked.

'No,' James said.

Ed looked round at Ketty – then, seeing she was asleep, glanced at me. Of course he didn't actually look me straight in the eye. Ed never does – says he can't help but mind-read you if he does that.

'What d'you think, Nico?' he asked.

'What choice do we have?' I said, thinking it through. 'A hotel's no safer than a private home. And if Foster's spy knew where we were going then there's no such thing as a "safe" house.'

Ed nodded and turned round.

Fifteen minutes later, James pulled the car across a crunchy gravel drive, I woke Ketty and we got out.

'Wow,' she said, looking at the tiny, detached brick cottage in front of us. 'It's like something off a postcard.'

It was. There were roses blooming all round the walls and flowering plants climbing up the front to two tiny latticed windows on the first floor. James fetched the key from its hiding place and unlocked the front door. It opened straight into a tiny living room, complete with armchairs, fireplace and the smell of damp.

Ed wandered over to Ketty, smoothing down his hair. Even though he'd been asleep, his chinos still had a neatly pressed line down the front. I shook my head as he told Ketty about our new plan – how we were going to stay here overnight and throw Foster off our trail. It was typical of Ed to try and take over like that. He went out with Ketty for a bit, you see, and part of me suspected he wished he still did.

As James and Maria took off their jackets and disappeared into the kitchen, Dylan drew me to one side.

'At least they're packing heat,' she whispered, pointing to James. Now that he'd taken his jacket off, the outline of a revolver was clearly visible under his shirt.

'Well that's a comfort,' I murmured.

I wanted to sound light and unbothered but, if I was honest, it *was* reassuring to know that our protectors were properly weaponed-up.

It turned out there were two bedrooms upstairs. 'One for the boys and one for the girls,' James said brightly. 'Though Maria and I are going to take turns keeping watch down here.'

Dylan and Ketty disappeared into their bedroom immediately, leaving the door ajar. I turned to Ed.

'Guess the girls reckon they need some beauty sleep.' I grinned.

'Don't you?' Ed raised his eyebrows as we walked into our room. It was tiny – just enough space for a chest of drawers under the window, with a narrow bed on either side.

'Nah,' I said. 'I'm good on just a few hours.'

'Oh, give it a rest,' Ed muttered. 'It's one thirty in the morning.' He flopped onto the bed on the right.

I sighed and wandered out onto the landing. Downstairs I could hear James and Maria whispering furiously, presumably trying not to disturb us. I poked my head round the girls' bedroom door. Their room was larger than mine and Ed's – but laid out in a similar way, with a double bed to the right of the door, a small sofa to the left and a window on the other side of the room.

Ketty was lying on the bed, still fully clothed. I could see from the way she was sprawled across the pillow that she was already asleep. Dylan had kicked off her shoes and was curled up on the sofa. She yawned as she looked up at me, her eyes glinting green in the light from the landing.

'Guess you'll have to wait 'til morning, loverboy,' she said with a grin.

'Whatever.' I wandered back out onto the landing. I didn't feel tired at all. Maria was coming up the stairs.

'Just going to check on the girls,' she said.

I nodded and padded downstairs.

James was pacing across the living room, a frown creasing his forehead.

He looked up when he saw me.

'Hi, Nico, you okay?'

'Yeah, I'm good.' I hesitated. 'What's going on? You look kind of worried.'

'It's nothing.' James smiled. 'We've agreed we'll just spend a few hours here, then Geri will tell us where to go next. If I were you, I'd get your head down.'

'I will. I'm gonna go outside for some air first though, okay?'

James hesitated for a second, then nodded. 'Just don't wander off.'

I slipped out the front door and crunched over the gravel to where a line of trees met the road. A car zoomed up the road. For a split second I froze. Could Foster have found us?

But the car didn't stop. I watched it disappear into the distance. Further along the road, I could just make out the brick walls of a couple more houses. It was pretty deserted here. I blew out my breath, watching it mist in the chilly night air.

In my bag upstairs, I'd packed a couple of pairs of jeans, spare trainers and a few T-shirts. The only other things with me were my iPod and a photo of my mum and my stepdad, Fergus. Like all our mums, mine died when I was little, from a virus connected with the Medusa gene. I don't remember her at all. After she died, I stayed with Fergus. He runs Fox Academy, where we're all at school, and knows all about the Medusa Project.

I'd hardly had time to say goodbye to him, what with the bomb alert and having to clear the school. I hoped he was safe, and not too worried about us all. For a second, I felt a stab of homesickness at the thought I wouldn't see him for such a long time. I shook it off and went back to the house.

I'd left the front door on the latch. As soon as I clicked it shut behind me, I knew something was wrong.

The house was too quiet. I glanced through the living room, into the kitchen. The lights were on in both rooms, but there was no sign of either James or Maria. Maybe they were both upstairs. Except . . . hadn't James said they were going to take it in turns to keep watch down here?

My throat felt dry as I strained to hear any sound from upstairs.

Nothing. I tiptoed uneasily up the stairs. The top step creaked. I held my breath, my heart pounding. Why was it so quiet?

For God's sake, man, they probably fell asleep.

I crept towards the room I was sharing with Ed. I pushed at the door. It opened slowly, with a creak.

Ed was no longer in his bed.

No.

No, no, no.

I stood on the landing, my mind running over what on earth could possibly have happened. Where *was* everyone? Had they all left while I wasn't looking? No, I'd have heard them on that crunchy gravel drive. Same if anyone had tried to get into the house from outside. There was no way Foster could have arrived without me noticing.

They *must* be here. Heart pounding, I glanced round for something to defend myself with, something I could teleport if I had to . . . The landing was empty, apart from a small table by the stairs containing a row of tiny silver-framed photos.

I raised my hand and teleported two of them into my palm.

Slowly, I pushed open the door to the girls' room.

A second of darkness, then a blinding light flashed in

my eyes. I squinted, turned away, tried to shield myself from the glare.

'Who are you?' I forced my voice to stay strong.

'Just stay there, Nico, and you'll be okay.' It was James.

I reached for the light switch by the door. I flicked it on. Nothing.

'James?' I said. 'What's going on?'

'Stay put,' James insisted. 'I'm serious. I've got a gun.'

I froze.

Why was James threatening me? He was here to protect us. Was someone else here? And where were the girls?

'What the hell are you doing?' I said.

'Wait by the door. Don't move.'

Still shielding my eyes from the light, I took a few hesitant steps, in the direction of the bed.

'Ketty?' I said. 'Dylan?'

No reply.

'Stand *still*,' James ordered.

My heart drummed against my chest. What was he doing? The light was still glaring in my eyes. I had to act. Work out what was going on.

Now.

I darted sideways, towards the sofa – the one Dylan had been curled up on. As I crashed onto it I realised she was still there. I'd landed on her legs.

She didn't move.

Man, what the hell was happening?

The glaring light followed me. But for a split second I

saw behind it. James was standing in the corner of the room, beside the window. The torch he'd been blinding me with was in his hand. He was alone.

It took a second for the full impact of this to sink in.

James was working against us. Against the Medusa Project.

Fury rose in me. 'What have you done to Dylan?' I yelled, hurling one of the silver photo frames towards the light.

James ducked to avoid it. As he moved, the torchlight wavered, giving me another second without the glare in my eyes. Squinting, I glanced over at the bed. Ketty and Ed were lying there, bound and gagged. Their eyes were shut and, like Dylan, they were completely still.

'Stay where you are and don't move,' James ordered.

Before I knew what was happening, he was rushing towards me, the torchlight brighter than ever . . . flaring in my eyes.

In one move James grabbed my wrist and dropped the torch. It fell with a thud onto the floor.

James yanked my arm behind my back. *Ow.* I gasped with the shock of the sudden pain.

'Get off!'

I still had one of the photo frames. With my free hand I drove it against James's head.

'Aaagh!' He reeled back.

I scrambled across the sofa, panting.

'What the hell are you doing?' I shouted at him.

'You're supposed to be looking after us.' I looked over at Ketty, lying so still on the bed. Was she unconscious? Worse?

'Slight change of plan, Nico.' James lunged for me.

He caught my arm and jerked it up behind me again. I struggled. He yanked my arm higher, breathing heavily with the effort. The force of the movement was so fierce I thought the pain would make me vomit.

For a second I stopped fighting. In an instant James had wound some sort of plastic rope round my wrists. He pulled it tight, then sat back, panting.

I focused on the binding, trying to loosen it telekinetically. It was impossible. There was no knot to untie. Whatever clasp was holding the plastic together was too powerful for me to unstick. I kicked out. James scrambled off the sofa and stood up.

'It's over, Nico. *Jesus*, I knew you'd be the hardest to control, but—'

'Why are you doing this?' I demanded, looking round for something to teleport at him. But the room was completely empty.

'Calm down.'

My heart pounded. I still couldn't take it in. I suddenly remembered the other agent who'd driven here with us.

'Maria?' I yelled.

'Be quiet.' James pulled a foul-smelling cloth out of his pocket. 'Maria's already out cold. This is just me.'

'What's that?'

He walked towards me. 'Nothing.' He grabbed my bound wrists and twisted them round and up. I fought against him as he brought the cloth up to my mouth.

'No.' I struggled, pressing my lips together. Whatever was on the cloth had to be some sort of drug. I glanced again at the others. He must have used this on them.

James pushed the cloth against my mouth. 'Give it up, Nico,' he said.

Desperate, I tried to hold my breath.

Shit.

I looked round. There must be something – *anything* – I could use as a weapon . . . I caught sight of Ketty's bag, poking out from underneath her bed.

Yes. With a roar I teleported it up and across the room. *Wham.* It rammed against James's side. Knocked him to the floor. I scrambled up, onto my feet. I raised the bag again, ready to dash it against him as he stood up.

'Put that down,' James ordered.

'No,' I said.

Then James raised his hand. He was holding a gun. He pointed it at me.

'Jesus, Nico, I don't want to use this, but I will if I have to,' he said. 'You have three seconds to put that bag down.'

'No!'

'Three . . .'

I focused on the gun, trying mentally to wrest it out of his hands, but he was gripping it too tightly.

'Two . . .' James shifted slightly, so the gun was now

pointing at the bed where Ed and Ketty lay. 'Lower the bag and close your eyes, or I'm shooting Ketty.'

My breath caught in my throat.

'One . . .'

I didn't have a choice.

I let the bag drop.

Ketty: dawn

'So, what are we going to do?' I asked.

Nico shook his head.

On the sofa, Ed chewed his lip. 'I can't believe James would *do* this,' he said.

'Well he has,' Nico said, shortly.

It was light outside – early morning – and we were still in the room I'd been sharing with Dylan. Ed and I were sitting on the bed, Nico and Dylan on the small sofa opposite.

We were all bound at the wrists and ankles. Nico and Ed were also blindfolded. Ed's hair stuck up in sandy tufts above the band round his eyes. It made him look even more vulnerable than usual. Unlike Nico, who somehow managed to look cool, even in his blindfold.

Dylan had been wearing tape over her mouth, but I'd managed to pick that off for her when I woke up.

'I guess we could yell,' Dylan suggested. 'Maybe if we were real loud the neighbours would hear.'

'The windows are double-glazed,' Nico pointed out.

'And the nearest neighbours are miles down the road – I saw last night when I went outside.'

I sighed. Last night was a blur for me – all I remembered was stumbling inside the cottage, then falling asleep on the bed. I'd half woken when Ed came in to say goodnight. After that I had a vague recollection of James's voice and a hand pressing damp gauze over my mouth. The smell of it had been horrible, but I'd had to breathe it in, and the next thing I remember was waking up with Ed lying next to me, drugged and tied up too – and the others in the same state on the sofa.

Now we were all awake. We must have been talking in low voices for ten minutes or so – there was no sign of either James or Maria. I'd managed, despite the plastic ties round my wrist, to reach the door and window handles, but both were locked.

'Why is James *doing* this? What's he after?' Ed asked.

'Maybe he's planning to hand us over to Foster,' Nico suggested.

Of course. I nodded. 'James must be the spy who's been giving Foster information on the Medusa Project,' I said.

'Forget *why* James is doing this,' Dylan said. 'The important thing is, how are we going to get away?'

I looked at my beautiful boyfriend. Nico's telekinesis had saved us before.

Saved my life.

'Can you untie our wrists and ankles, Nico?' I asked.

'No.' He made a face. 'This stuff James used has got some sort of plastic seal. And unless I can get my blindfold off I won't be able to teleport anything either,' Nico said. 'I have to see what I want to move – or at least feel it – first.'

'And I can't mind-read anyone unless I can see into their eyes,' Ed added.

I gazed at their blindfolds. It struck me that James had only met us a couple of times – and had certainly never seen us in action. He must have really studied our files to be able to limit our abilities so precisely.

'What about you, Dylan?'

She tossed her head, flicking her long red hair out of her eyes. 'I can protect myself from most sorts of attack, but not if it comes at me real hard or real fast. And being tied up makes it hard to help anyone else.'

'It's like James knows exactly what we're capable of,' I said.

'And he's stopping us from doing it.' Dylan nodded.

'He might have stopped the rest of us,' Ed said, slowly, 'but you could still have a vision, Ketty.'

'Yeah.' Dylan's voice grew excited.

'Ketty?' Nico said. 'What d'you think?'

I swallowed. I'd only just started being able to bring on visions at will – apart from the three people in this room, only Geri knew I could do it – and I didn't find it easy. Especially in front of the others, who seemed so competent and capable when it came to handling their powers.

'I'll give it a go,' I said uncertainly. 'But I'm not sure how it'll help. I still can't really control what I see.'

I turned my face to the window, where the light was brightest. I blinked rapidly, trying to jump-start a vision. Lights flashed in front of my eyes. *Keep going.* I carried on blinking, trying not to think about how I looked. Dylan had once told me I looked freaky when I had visions. At least with that blindfold on Nico couldn't see me.

The lights were really flashing now. A sweet sickly perfume filled the air. The vision rose up . . .

Nico by the sea. Waves crashing on a cold beach. All of us there. I'm looking at Nico. He's staring at someone else. Not Ed or Dylan. I can't see who. His dark brown eyes are angry. 'You're the real *thief,' Nico says.*

I snapped out of the vision

'What happened?' Dylan leaped in. 'What did you see?'

'Give her a chance.' That was Nico.

Heart sinking, I told them what I'd seen. 'Sorry,' I said, feeling that I'd let them down. 'Sorry, it's not much help.'

'We don't know that, yet,' Ed said. 'We don't know what will help and what won't.'

Dylan snorted. 'Well, Nico on a beach isn't going to get these bindings off, is it?'

'At least Ketty's seen that we *are* going to get them off,' Nico said, darkly.

Footsteps sounded outside. The door swung open. It was James.

'Sleep well?' he said.

'You drugged us,' Dylan snarled.

'What are you going to do with us?' Nico demanded.

James looked round at us. He was wearing the same clothes as yesterday – jeans and a leather jacket. His hair didn't look quite so gelled up as before, though, and there were dark shadows under his eyes.

'I'm sorry about drugging you,' he said, leaning against the door frame. 'But you're too powerful to take any risks with.'

'What've you done with Maria?' Ed asked.

'She's tied up downstairs,' James said. 'She's got nothing to do with this.'

My guts gave a sickening twist. Poor Maria.

'Are you working for Foster?' I said.

James smiled. 'Foster has no idea where you are,' he said. 'That was just a cover story so you wouldn't get suspicious when we took a detour.'

I caught Dylan's eye. She looked as surprised as I felt. What James was doing *wasn't* connected with Foster? Then what was going on?

'What about the training camp?' I said, confused. 'Why aren't we going there?'

'You are,' James went on. 'I'm just borrowing you for the day first.'

'*Borrowing* us?' Dylan held up her bound wrists. 'Don't you mean kidnapping us?'

'Borrowing us to do what?' Nico demanded.

James smiled again. 'To steal diamonds,' he said.

'*What?*' Nico said.

James crossed his arms. 'A wealthy friend of my mother's – a *very* wealthy friend – owns some extremely expensive diamonds. They're set in various pieces of jewellery which she keeps in a safe at her house,' James explained. 'Altogether the diamonds are worth over five million pounds. And I want them.'

'Well, go and get them,' Dylan said. 'You've got a gun. Get this woman to give you the diamonds.'

'I can't do that. For one thing Mrs Carter and her husband know me. For another, I happen to know that part of the insurance requirement for covering the diamonds is a security measure over which they have no direct control. *I* won't be able to bypass it. But *you* will.'

I thought back to my vision of Nico on the beach. *You're the* real *thief*, he'd said. It must have been James he'd been talking to.

Nico whistled. 'So you want *us* to steal them for you?'

'Yes,' James said with a smile.

Ed shook his head. 'But that doesn't make sense. You're connected with us. Once we've been identified, Geri Paterson will ask questions and work out you were behind the whole thing – and you'll be arrested.'

He was right. Geri Paterson was the head of the Medusa Project – the woman who had brought the four of us together and who was now sending us to a training camp for two months. She had phenomenal power over the authorities. There was no way she wouldn't find out – and fast – if we stole a bunch of diamonds.

'No one will identify you,' James said. 'And even if the Carters offer up a few clues, the police won't connect you with the crime.'

'Why not?' I asked.

'The police can't track and arrest people who no longer exist,' he said, matter-of-factly.

'No longer exist?' What did *that* mean?

'If it was a bigger crime than theft, then there might be a small risk of some high-ranking officers working it out, but lower down the food chain . . .' James waved his hand impatiently. 'Anyway, that doesn't matter right now. All you need to know is how to steal the diamonds.'

I stared at him, my skin bursting into goosebumps. How could we no longer exist? Was he was planning to *kill* us?

Nico was obviously thinking the same thing. 'Geri'll never let it go if we don't turn up at this training camp,' he said.

'You *will* turn up,' James said. 'Just one day later than planned.'

'This is ridiculous,' Nico said. 'You can't *make* us take the diamonds. I mean, if you hurt us we won't be able to steal them.'

'That's true.' James's voice was icy. 'I'm not going to hurt *you*, Nico – or Dylan or Ed. Not the three I *need*. But if you don't do what I say and keep quiet about it, I *will* hurt Ketty.'

I gasped. 'Me?'

'Yes.' James's eyes burned into mine. 'You. You're the least useful member of the team – at least as far as I'm concerned. The others' silence buys your safety. It's as simple as that.'

I glanced at Nico. The blindfold hid most of his smooth, olive-skinned face but his lips were pressed so tightly together they were white.

'If you *dare* touch Ketty—'

'I won't have to, Nico,' James said calmly. 'Not if everyone does what I tell them.'

My heart pounded.

'So what's to stop us telling someone what you've made us do *afterwards* . . . once we get to the camp?' Dylan demanded.

Ed nodded. 'What's to stop *Maria* saying something? You can't keep her tied up forever.'

'Maria will keep quiet for the same reason that the rest of you will.' He turned to me. 'Like I said, it's all about *you*, Ketty. It's obvious that both Ed and Nico would do anything to protect you.'

I looked away, my face flushing.

'On top of which, you and Dylan are friends and I know Maria has a soft spot for you,' James went on. 'If anyone breathes a word *after* the theft takes place, I swear I will make it my life's ambition to hunt you down and kill you.'

A terrible silence fell over the room as James let this threat hang in the air.

I stared at the floor, unable to look at any of the others.

James stood up. 'Come on, Ketty, let's go.'

'*No!*' Nico said. 'Stop!'

'*Please*, James,' Ed pleaded.

'Where are you taking me?' I asked, trying to keep my voice steady.

James took a knife from his pocket. He held it towards me.

I gasped.

'Leave her alone,' Dylan yelled.

James knelt and in a single swift move cut through the binding round my ankles. I got to my feet, my legs trembling.

'If you hurt her, I'll be the one hunting *you* down,' Nico shouted. 'Frigging arsehole.'

'I'll be okay, Nico,' I said. Whatever was going to happen, the last thing I wanted was Nico provoking James into hurting *him*.

James gripped my arm and led me outside and down the stairs. As we crossed the living room I glanced at the kitchen. Maria was sitting on a chair, rope tied round her body.

'Ketty, help!' she cried out. 'He's going to kill me.'

'Shut up!' James swore, kicking the kitchen door shut.

He dragged me over to the front door and shoved me outside. Tears pricked at my eyes. How could this be happening? I'd spent the last few days consumed with worry about my brother Lex, trying to rescue him from Foster.

And now, just when I thought everything was going to be okay, here was a new threat . . . a new danger.

It was cold in the bright morning air, the sky dull and overcast. I shivered.

James walked over to the huge people carrier we'd travelled here in the night before.

I looked round, desperate to find something that might help me get away. I could only see a short way up the road in either direction. Like Nico had said, the nearest house was miles away.

James unlocked the car.

'Where are we going?' I said.

'We're not going anywhere.' He opened the boot. 'Say hello to your home for the next few hours.'

I stared inside. It was fairly large, but surely once the boot door shut it would be dark – and airless.

'I won't be able to breathe,' I said, panicking, backing away.

'You'll be fine,' James snapped. 'I'll come back out in an hour or so with some water. Now, get in.'

I stared at him. He couldn't be serious. 'You don't have to do this,' I pleaded. 'You can just shut me in another room.'

'It's better if the others don't know where you are,' he said, half pulling his gun out of his pocket. 'Plus, I don't want you overhearing anything,' He shoved me towards the car. 'Come on, hurry up!'

A chill snaked down my spine as I realised how closely

James must have studied my file. He knew exactly what I was capable of, and what I wasn't – I couldn't have a vision of a place or time I didn't experience. And if I wasn't involved in the jewellery theft, then I wouldn't be able to foresee it . . .

Shaking, I climbed into the boot. James bound my mouth and legs again and then, without speaking, he slammed the boot shut.

I was trapped and alone.

Ed: midday

James marched us out of the house and into his car. Nico, Dylan and I were all blindfolded and gagged. Most of James's attention was on Nico, which meant I kept stumbling and bumping into things. Still, who cared about a few bruises . . . there was only one thing on my mind.

Ketty. Where was she? What had he done with her? If only James would take this blindfold off, I could mind-read him and find out.

James shoved us onto the back seats of his 4x4 and told us to lie down, then covered us with a blanket. I lay in the dark, with one of Dylan's shoes against my face as the car drove away. Five minutes later we turned onto a bumpy road. The car pulled to a stop. I felt the blanket covering us being whisked off and struggled to sit up. It was lighter behind my blindfold now – not that I could make out anything beyond a red glow. My wrists were sore from where the plastic binding cut into my skin.

James pulled the gags off our mouths.

'Okay.' He cleared his throat. 'Survive the ride?'

'Yeah, we're great,' Nico muttered. 'Now will you frigging untie us, please?'

'In a minute.'

I wriggled in my seat. I was uncomfortable and sweaty, my hair sticking to my forehead. A trickle of perspiration tickled my cheek but I couldn't reach to wipe it away.

Like Ketty had said, James knew exactly what we were capable of and how to control our powers.

Ketty. It hurt inside my chest when I thought about her. She was my best friend – and she could be anywhere, scared or badly hurt . . . or worse . . .

'Right, now I'm going to explain how you're going to get past Mr Carter and the security in the safe he can't control,' James said.

'We won't be getting past anyone if you don't untie my hands and take this blindfold off,' Nico snapped. 'And where the hell is Ketty?'

'Yes . . . *Please* tell us she's okay.' I could hear how anxious I sounded. 'She *is* okay, isn't she?'

'I was just coming to Ketty,' James said curtly. 'Now, listen. In a minute I'm going to untie you. Remember, if you try anything, you'll never see Ketty again. A friend of mine's with her. I don't even know where he's taken her, so there's no point mind-reading me, Ed, but unless he hears from me every ten minutes, he's got instructions to kill her. Do you understand?'

'Er . . . yes,' I said, my heart racing. I could barely focus on what James was saying. I closed my eyes behind my blindfold, trying to steady my nerves.

'Okay,' Nico muttered.

'Deal,' Dylan said.

'Right.' James paused. Then he explained the plan.

I calmed down a little as he spoke. I had to admit the plan was clever. And simple. Each of us had a role . . . each of us was needed to make the robbery work. We sat in silence, listening as he went over what we had to do.

'Any questions?' James asked, finally.

'Just one,' Nico said. 'Did you train to be this much of an arsehole, or does it come naturally?'

'Shut up,' James snapped.

For God's sake. Why did Nico have to be so antagonistic? I hadn't liked James right from the start, with his oily hair and mean little eyes, but being rude to him wasn't going to help Ketty. Nico was her boyfriend. He was supposed to *care* about her, not endanger her by getting all aggressive with the guy who was holding her captive.

'Okay, time to go.' James reached over, grabbed my wrists and sliced through the binding. Then he yanked off my blindfold.

I blinked at the brightness of the light and rubbed my sore wrists. As James released the others I looked round. We were parked in a narrow country lane, just off a bigger, tarmac road. A couple of cars whizzed along the road. I couldn't see any pedestrians.

James turned to face me. He was wearing dark sunglasses, clearly taking no chances that I might attempt to mind-read him.

'Here.' Holding his gun in one hand, he shoved a balaclava at me with the other, then pointed to a tiny black dot just beside the left eyehole.

'There's one of these for each of you,' he explained. 'The dot is a fibre-optic camera and microphone. My eyes and ears while you're in the Carters' house. Roll down the masks once you get to the drive. It's just a few yards round the corner.'

I tugged the balaclava on, then rolled up the sides so it looked like a beanie hat. Seconds later we were out of the car and racing up the country lane.

Half a minute later we reached the house. It was enormous. A gravel drive, lined with tall trees, led up to a four-storey brick mansion. Just one car – a sleek silver Bentley – was parked outside the front door.

'So far so good,' Dylan whispered, as we pulled down our balaclavas.

I nodded. James had already explained Mr Carter would be alone in the house – his wife was always at the hairdresser's this time of the week.

Nico was already focusing on the front door, his hands held over the handle. With a click, the lock retracted and the door swung back.

He glanced sideways at me and Dylan. 'We're in,' he muttered.

Making sure I left the front door open – part of James's plan to make the robbery look opportunistic – I followed the others into the house. The hallway was brightly lit, but still had an old, slightly musty smell. My heart thumped as we crept across the wooden floor, past a living room full of dark wood panelling and chintz-covered furniture.

James thought that the safe containing Mrs Carter's jewellery would be somewhere near the master bedroom, but our first job was to find her husband. As we reached the stairs, Nico held his finger to his lips. We stood, silently, listening.

Footsteps sounded above us. Nico pointed up the stairs, then began to climb them. Dylan followed. I tiptoed after them, feeling weak at the knees.

As we reached the first-floor landing, a door opened along the corridor ahead of us. And then several things happened at once.

An elderly man, with grey hair and a stooped back, walked out into the corridor. His eyes just had time to register horror, and then Nico was at his side, hissing in his ear.

Dylan raced over. I turned away, unable to watch. This was *so* wrong. It was bad enough having psychic abilities in the first place, but using them to make some poor old man give up his wife's diamonds was worse than evil. If Ketty's life wasn't at stake there was no way I'd let myself be used like this. *No way.*

'Oy, Chino Boy, get down here,' Dylan yelled at me.

I stumbled down the corridor towards them. I barely noticed Dylan's insult. I felt strangely numb, like all this wasn't really happening.

Mr Carter's face was lined and grey. He pressed himself against the wall behind him as I got closer. Dylan and Nico each held one of his arms.

I stopped, a metre or so away, feeling sick.

'You're up.' Nico grabbed my arm, and shoved me in front of Mr Carter. I could feel the fear radiating off the old man. I bit my lip. The balaclava prickled against my mouth.

'What do you want?' Mr Carter's voice was quavery.

I took a deep breath and looked into his eyes.

In an instant, I was there . . . inside his mind. The first, panicky wave of his thoughts broke over me.

What's happening? What are you doing? What do you want?

It's all right, I made myself think-speak. I always try to be as calm as possible when it's someone's first time. I guess it's scary for them. When I'm inside someone's head they're basically paralysed – unable to speak or move unless I let them, or until I break the connection.

I waited for the old man's thoughts to settle a bit, but they kept jumping around. One moment he'd be thought-speaking to me. The next, his own private thoughts forced their way to the front of his mind.

Please don't hurt me. ***Hooligan element.*** *I've got grandchildren.* ***What's happening?*** *I've been ill. How are* *you doing this?* ***Lord, will they hurt me? Hooligans.*** *What do you want?*

'Hurry up.' Nico's voice sounded impatiently in my ear.

Please calm down, Mr Carter, I thought-spoke again, very slowly and deliberately. *I just want to know where the diamonds are.*

What? No! ***In the safe.*** *No . . . They're mine . . . Cheryl's . . .* ***The safe*** *. . .*

Good. I wasn't going to have to probe too deeply into Mr Carter's mind. It's funny how the very things people try not to focus on are exactly what jump to the front of their minds.

Okay, so the diamonds are in the safe. Where's the safe? Is it on this floor?

No . . . no . . . no . . . ***yes . . . master bedroom . . . dressing room . . . left . . . left of the dressing table*** *. . . no . . . no . . .*

I called out the information. Footsteps rushed away. Dylan, going to investigate.

I'm sorry, Mr Carter. We're not going to hurt you. I tried to make my thought-speech sound as gentle as possible. Several long seconds passed. I kept the connection, trying not to engage with Mr Carter's panic-stricken thoughts.

'I've found the safe,' Dylan called out. 'What's the combination?'

The safe combination, Mr Carter?

No . . . can't tell you . . . don't know . . . don't know . . .

Damn, the old man had clearly realised how my telepathy worked. He was making a big effort to stop himself from consciously thinking the numbers of the safe combination.

I sighed.

'*Ed*,' Nico hissed in my ear. 'Get *on* with it.'

Sorry, Mr Carter. I drew in my breath to focus, then dived into the first level of his deeper thoughts. They were all muddled up, like most people's. Memories of a wedding day swirling around; his (not particularly flattering) opinion about what Mrs Carter had cooked for supper last night; and a persistent, nagging desire to complain about a mail order delivery of red wine. I pushed a little harder. It's difficult to explain what that feels like – but it doesn't usually take long to find something once the person you're mind-reading knows you're after it.

Imagine, for instance, that you and I were speaking and I said to you, *Don't think about a penguin in a red hat.* Isn't a penguin in a red hat *exactly* what you're going to think about?

There. I found the part of Mr Carter's mind which held the combination. I shouted the sequence out to Dylan.

'Left 28 . . . right 11 . . . left 44 . . . it's his wife's birthday . . .'

'Fascinating,' Nico muttered. 'Are we done?'

'Yes,' I said.

There was a short pause.

You still won't be able to get into the safe . . . Oh, dear

God, what are you going to do to me? Please don't hurt me. Mr Carter's thought-speech felt like he was sobbing.

My guts twisted. *Don't worry, Mr Carter, please – you're going to be fine.*

In the distance I could hear faint clicking noises as Dylan released the safe. I kept my gaze firmly on Mr Carter's eyes in case we needed more information, but I stayed at the surface level of his thoughts.

'Whoa, this is *sooo* awesome,' Dylan shouted out. 'I can see the diamonds, they're *enormous*.'

'What about the force field?' Nico asked.

I could feel Mr Carter's mind tense up at this.

How does the other boy know about that? he thought-spoke.

I swallowed, trying to ignore his question. James had explained when he'd briefed us that the safe contained a state-of-the art laser force field that was linked directly to an alarm at the local police station. The Carters had no direct control over it at home.

James had also warned it would burn the skin of anyone reaching through it to the diamonds.

Any normal person.

'Yeah, the force field's here,' Dylan shouted. 'I'm putting my hand in now. I can feel it but it's not hurting. *Whoa*, the laser's going round my hand . . . *awesome* . . . the stream isn't even broken. *No* problem.'

'Just get the frigging diamonds, will you?' Nico shouted.

How is she doing that? Why isn't the alarm going off?

I ignored Mr Carter's thought-speech. Even if I explained about Dylan's ability to withstand physical attack, I was pretty sure he wouldn't be able to get his head round it.

Seconds later, there was a rustling sound and then Dylan was back. 'Got them.'

'Okay,' Nico ordered. 'Time to go.'

Thanks, Mr Carter. You're going to be fine.

What's this? What's he putting over my mouth? ***Smells ghastly****. Please don't . . . please . . .* Mr Carter's pitiful thoughts faded. His eyes glazed as his mind stilled into unconsciousness.

I broke the eye-to-eye contact and stood back.

Nico eased Mr Carter onto the floor. The drugged handkerchief James had given him was still clamped around the old man's mouth.

'How long did James say that would put him out for?' I asked anxiously.

'Not long.' Nico glanced at me. 'This sucks big time, doesn't it?'

I nodded, still staring at the old man. He looked so helpless, lying there on the floor.

Dylan was already at the top of the stairs, a small velvet bag in her hand. She pulled her balaclava off.

'Come *on*,' she called. 'Let's get out of here.'

'Okay, just wait a sec.' I darted into the nearest room –

some kind of office. I grabbed a cushion off the chair at the desk, ran back and eased it under Mr Carter's head.

'Very nice . . . very caring . . .' Nico said, his tone half amused, half exasperated. 'Now, come on. Let's give James these frigging diamonds and get Ketty back.'

I followed him down the stairs and out of the front door, tugging my balaclava off as I ran. We jogged round the corner. The car was parked in the same place. James was sitting in the font seat, still wearing his dark glasses. He reached over and opened the front passenger door.

I raced over. 'Where's Ketty?' I demanded.

'Get in,' James said, roughly. His gun was gripped tightly in his hand.

Nico ran up. 'Not 'til you tell us where Ketty is.'

'We've got the diamonds.' Dylan held out the bag.

'I know.' James swore. 'Stop flashing them about and get in the bloody car.'

The others scrambled into the back seat. James held out two blindfolds. 'Put these on,' he ordered, still gripping his gun.

I watched him, knowing he was holding the gun too tightly for Nico to teleport it away.

'Get in, Ed,' James said.

'What about Ketty?'

'My friend's looking after Ketty, remember?' James snapped. 'I'll call him once we've got away from here.'

'No.' I stood stubbornly on the pavement. It's funny. The Medusa gene that's inside each of us has developed in a different way according to our personalities. I don't know for certain why I ended up able to mind-read, but I reckon it's got something to do with the fact that, unless I'm *really* feeling messed up, like I was earlier, I have good instincts. For instance, I can almost always sense when people are lying to me. And, right now, I was sure that what James had just said about Ketty being with his friend wasn't true.

I glanced into the car, where Nico was holding the blindfold in his hand like it was a dirty hanky. He felt my gaze and looked up. *Whoosh.* I jumped into his mind.

Sunglasses, I demanded. *Get James's sunglasses.*

I broke the connection. Nico turned. Held up his hands. In an instant the sunglasses were off James's face and soaring into Nico's outstretched palms.

Instinctively, James reached for them. Before he had time to realise what I was doing and shield his eyes, I was inside the car and across the passenger seat.

Trying not to think about the gun in his hand, I grabbed his chin and turned his head to face mine.

Connection. I dived in through James's eyes.

Where's Ketty? I demanded. *What have you done with her?*

James was trying to push my thoughts away but I forced my way further into his head. *God, what a mess.* A jumble of incoherent emotions. Rage. The diamond stealing plan going round and round in his head. *Will it work . . .? Can it work . . .?* and fear. Blood-curdling anxiety that he would be caught. That we would overpower him.

Ketty! I demanded.

There. I saw what he knew about our abilities . . . *yes*. I saw where Ketty was. And . . . and *what the hell was that?*

I broke the connection, unable to believe what I'd just stumbled across.

As soon as I let go of James's mind, he started shouting.

'Let me go, you little bastards.'

I blinked, taking in for the first time that Dylan had got out of the car and was now standing in the road, reaching over James in the driver's seat and fastening his wrists with the same plastic binding he'd used on us. His ankles were already tied.

Nico wound one of the blindfolds round James's mouth, as I scrambled out of the car. My head was whirling with what I'd seen. I needed some air.

Nico looked anxiously over at me as he pushed James down into the space between the front seats and the steering panel. Dylan had grabbed James's legs and was tying them to the accelerator pedal. She took his gun and held it carefully between her fingers. Nico fastened James's wrists to the bar under the front passenger seat, then jumped out of the car and grabbed my shoulders.

'What happened?' he asked. 'What did you see? Is Ketty all right?'

'Yeah,' I said, still feeling dazed. 'She's in the boot.'

'*What?*' Nico raced to the back of the car. I could hear

him clicking the boot open. Ketty's wail as he pulled her gag off. His voice, suddenly soft and reassuring.

He was holding her . . . hugging her . . . comforting her . . .

I stood, staring down at the pavement, unable to move. Dylan walked round the car and came up beside me. I could feel her gaze on my face – those pale green eyes piercing through me.

'What's up?' she said. 'Awesome move on the bad guy, by the way.'

I nodded as Nico and Ketty came over. Ketty's face was tear-stained and creased from where she'd been lying in the boot of the car. She was holding on to Nico like he might suddenly fly off the pavement. But, for once, I didn't feel a stab of jealousy.

'We need to go,' Nico said. 'Get to a phone. Call Geri.'

I nodded, feeling numb.

'What is it, Ed?' Ketty asked.

I took a deep breath. 'It's just something I saw . . .' I hesitated, not wanting to say it out loud.

'*What* did you see?' Dylan asked, impatiently. James's gun still dangled from her hand.

'D'you remember James saying earlier that we no longer existed?' I said.

The others nodded.

'Well, it's true.'

'What?' Nico stared at me.

Ketty frowned. 'What do you mean?'

'All our records – school, medical, everywhere on paper and online – according to James's thoughts, they've all been wiped, or changed to say we're dead.'

'All four of us?' Dylan asked. 'Are you sure? Is James sure?'

'Yes. In James's mind us being listed as dead is not a belief or an opinion. It's a fact. It's the *truth*.'

'All the more reason to phone Geri fast,' Nico said. 'Find out what's going on.'

'It's gotta be part of James's plan,' Dylan said.

She opened the cylinder at the side of the gun and tipped the bullets out. I stared at her. How did she know how to do that? She saw me looking and grinned.

'James must reckon he can cover our tracks better if he's made out we're dead,' Nico said. 'He talked about it last night: how the police won't be able to connect us with the crime.'

'I don't know.' Ketty frowned. 'How would James have had time to get into all our records to fake our deaths *and* do everything else he's done today?'

'And why?' I asked. 'Isn't it more likely that he's planning to . . . to . . .'

'To kill us?' Dylan asked.

'But *why*?' I glanced back at the car where James lay, all trussed up. 'I suppose I could go back and read his mind again.'

'There's no time,' Nico insisted. 'Come *on*. Let's find a phone and—'

'We have to go back for Maria,' Ketty said suddenly. 'She's trapped in that house. James tied her up. I saw her on my way out.'

I was still preoccupied with us being listed as dead. 'So, before, when James said—'

'Will you stop going on about James!' Nico snapped. 'Ketty's right. We have to go back for Maria. The house can't be that far away. We were only driving for a few minutes. Do any of you remember the route we took?'

'I'm sure we took a left into this lane, which means we drove up there.' Dylan pointed down the tarmac road.

'And before we got onto that road, when we left the house, I remember sensing us turn left and then take a right, really quick, one after the other.' Nico said. 'We just have to retrace our steps. Get back to the house. Release Maria. Call Geri. Everything'll be sorted out in ten minutes. Come on.'

He broke into a run. Dylan raced after him.

I hesitated. Ketty grabbed my hand and gave it a tug.

'Ed, we need to hurry.'

Why was everyone always telling me to hurry?

'I'm coming,' I said. 'I just want to think this through.'

Ketty shifted impatiently from foot to foot. 'There really isn't anything to think through. The faster we go, the sooner we'll be able to call for help.'

I guessed she was right – and yet I still couldn't make sense of it. Why would James bother to list us as dead? It seemed a bit of an extreme length to go to, just to cover up one jewellery theft . . .

'Ed, come *on.*' Ketty raced off.

I gave up trying to figure it out and followed her.

Seven minutes later we panted up to the house.

Nico was about to start unlocking the front door using telekinesis, but then Dylan broke the windowpane and twisted her hand round to flip the catch.

The look on Nico's face was priceless. I smiled at that – even though everything was so tense. It's always good to see the wind taken out of Nico's sails.

We ran into the house.

'Maria was in the kitchen,' Ketty gasped.

As she raced across the living room, the kitchen door opened. Maria stood there, her mouth open in a huge 'O' shape. Her earrings jangled as she looked round at each of us in turn.

'How did you . . .? Where's . . .? What happened . . .?'

'How did you get free?' Dylan asked.

Maria blinked. 'It took me ages – nearly sliced my hands off with the kitchen knife. I literally just managed it. Are you guys all right?'

'Yeah.' Dylan handed her the gun and bullets. 'Have this. I hate guns.'

'Wait.' Everything was moving too fast. I knew something was wrong. 'How come we didn't see you when we left the house?'

'James drugged me after I called out to Ketty,' Maria said quickly. 'So, did you get the diamonds? How did you get away from James?' She started loading the gun

Dylan had just given her. 'This is James's gun. Where is he?'

'Tied up in his car.' Nico frowned. 'So if you got yourself free, how come you haven't called the police or Geri?'

'I told you.' Maria weighed the gun in her hand. 'I literally just this minute got free.'

'You're lying,' I said.

The others stared at me. Then Maria lifted the gun and pointed it at me. A slow smile spread across her face.

'Yes, Ed,' she said. 'You're right. I am.'

Dylan: sunset

The boat rocked and swayed. Ed's face underneath his blindfold was tinged with green.

'He needs some air,' Ketty said.

'No shit.' I looked round the cabin. It was a bedroom – but tiny. The sort you often get on small boats, with a cupboard in the corner and a tiny, locked porthole on one wall. The three of us were sitting on the bed, hands and ankles tied as before. Ed was the only one blindfolded.

He gave a groan and bowed his head in his hands.

'We *have* to get out of here,' I said, for about the hundredth time.

We'd been locked in this cabin for a couple of hours now. It was early evening – the light outside was fading and the sky, or at least as much of it as I could make out through the porthole, was dark grey and threatening a storm.

'D'you think Nico's all right?' Ketty said, also for about the hundredth time.

'I've no freakin' idea,' I snapped.

Ketty turned away like I'd slapped her face. *Crap*.

'Please, can't we all get on?' Ed said, plaintively. 'This is bad enough without everyone falling out.'

I dug my nails into my palms, hard, so as not to bite his head off too.

I was real mad at myself. I should have guessed Maria was in on the whole thing. James was so aware of our abilities, it made total sense he and Maria would have set up some kind of double bluff. And if I hadn't been in such a rush to give Maria that gun, there was no way she would have been able to get all four of us tied up while she went to fetch James.

I was also worried about Nico. Not that I'd admit it to anyone. All we knew was that he was somewhere else on the boat.

If only there was something I could do, but my ability is defensive. I can protect myself from physical attack, but it's kind of a passive skill. It only works if I'm in actual danger.

Nico's telekinesis was a much bigger threat to James and Maria and they knew it.

'I'm taking no bloody chances with this one,' James had more or less spat, before dragging Nico off and leaving Maria to lock the rest of us in this cabin.

'Where d'you think the boat's going?' Ed said quietly.

I got the distinct impression his question was for Ketty, not me.

'I don't know, but I've been thinking about what you

saw in James's mind,' Ketty said. 'About us being listed as dead. We need to find out what it means.'

'It's obvious what it freakin' means,' I said. 'It means he's planning to kill us and tell Geri we died on the way to the training camp.'

There was a long silence.

'I don't see why James would bother to list us as dead *before* he killed us. I mean, what's the point? And don't you think it's all a bit extreme – killing four people just for a few diamonds?' Ed said at last. 'I mean, I know they're worth a lot of money, but, before, James said he was taking us on to training camp after we'd stolen—'

'Of course he did, jerkwad,' I said. 'He wasn't going to *tell* us he was going to kill us, was he?'

'But we don't know for sure . . .' Ed persisted.

'Well, if you'd seen a bit more when you were mind-reading him then we *would* freakin' know for sure, wouldn't we?'

'Dylan, will you *please* calm down?' Ketty jumped up off the bed. 'It's not fair to get cross with Ed. He was doing the best he—'

'Yeah, yeah, all right. Stop freakin' whining,' I said. Then I hesitated. 'Sorry, Ed.'

He shrugged. We sat in silence again. I kicked my bound heels against the bed. Ketty shuffled over to the porthole. She stood on tiptoes and peered out.

'I can see land. We must be coming into dock.'

'Thank goodness for that,' Ed muttered. 'Five more minutes at sea and I'd definitely be sick.'

What a loser.

'This could be our best chance,' I said, ignoring him. 'They can't march us through a port all tied up, with Nico and Ed wearing blindfolds. They'll have to untie us. And once we're free, maybe Nico can get the gun off them and we can get away.'

'I don't think this *is* a port,' Ketty said from the window.

The boat's engine slowed to a crawl. I joined Ketty at the little porthole. It was raining outside now, the sky the colour of steel. The beach shoreline in front of us stretched as far as I could see, though that wasn't more than fifty yards or so. There were a few cottages in the distance but no sign of a port or a dock.

'Oh, crap,' I said.

'Where are we?' Ed asked from the bed.

'Could be anywhere,' Ketty said. 'Somewhere along the coast in England, maybe, or France, or even Holland.'

'No way.' I stared at her. I find British geography *real* confusing. 'Europe's that close?'

'Yup.' Ketty gritted her teeth.

I nodded. I like the way Ketty doesn't waste words. The way she keeps it real. I mean, she dresses like a hobo, but she knows who she is and what she wants.

The sound of a key turning in the lock made us both turn round. As Maria walked in, I realised that we still had no plan.

Maria stood in the doorway, all blonde highlights, skinny jeans and stupid earrings. I should have known she was one of the bad guys from that awesomely tasteless jewellery. What a *bitch*. Giving us all that training back at school, seeming like she really cared about us, then this . . .

'Time to go,' Maria said.

'Where are we?' I demanded.

'Where's Nico?' Ketty added.

'Er . . . have you got a bucket?' That was Ed.

I shot him a look. Of the four of us, Ed *would* be the one to get seasick. He's kind of annoying – the type of person I usually want to slap. But right now he looked real pale, like he genuinely was about to barf.

Maria clearly thought the same. 'Okay, Ed, you first. Over here, please.'

Ed shuffled slowly across the room.

'You could at least take his blindfold off,' I insisted.

'When we're outside.'

With one eye on Ketty and me, Maria bent down and sliced through Ed's ankle binding. She pushed him through the cabin, then beckoned Ketty over.

A few minutes later our feet were all untied, though our wrists were still bound behind our backs. Maria led us up on deck. The misty drizzle was damp on my face. I looked round, hoping to see something helpful, like a potential weapon, or a passing adult we could appeal to for help. But the deck was empty and the beach stretched into woods on either side. Apart from the cottages in the distance, there was no sign of human life at all.

'How can you do this to us, Maria?' Ketty asked.

Ignoring her, Maria donned a pair of shades and removed Ed's blindfold. It was dusk now, wherever we were, and gloomy with all the clouds. It suddenly struck me that Maria's ultra-black sunnies would make everything around her look even darker. Maybe I could make her limited vision work to our advantage. I gritted my teeth. If I couldn't use my psychic gift, at least I could be smart about more conventional ways of getting out of danger.

Maria ordered Ketty to jump off the little boat onto the wooden landing board that poked out into the sea. As she pushed Ketty forward, her attention turned away from me and Ed. I nudged Ed's arm.

He got it straight away for once . . . looked me directly in the eyes.

Dylan?

You go next. When you get onto shore, tell Ketty to wait for my signal, then do something to get Maria's attention.

What? Ed's voice inside my head had a note of panic about it. *What signal? Do* what *to get attention?*

'Over here, Dylan,' Maria called.

Shit. Ed broke the connection. 'Let Ed go first,' I said quickly. 'He's still feeling real seasick.'

'Fine.'

'Go.' I nudged Ed again.

He stumbled forwards, to the edge of the deck. Maria directed him to jump down. He landed heavily beside Ketty.

'Your turn.' Maria turned to me.

'Sure.' I tossed my head to get my hair off my face and moved towards her, watching Ed. He glanced for a split second into Ketty's eyes, communicating my message, then collapsed onto the sand with a groan.

'Aaagh . . . my leg . . .' He clutched his ankle, sounding surprisingly convincing.

'What?' Maria shouted, turning back to the beach. 'For God's sake, what's the matter?'

'I hurt my ankle when I fell,' Ed moaned.

I was right beside Maria now, on the edge of the boat. I took a last look round. No sign of James or Nico. The handle of the knife Maria had used to cut our ankle bindings was peeking out of her pocket. I turned sideways on to her, so my fingertips brushed against the knife handle. Sweat beaded on my forehead.

'Ed's really hurt,' Ketty called out from the beach.

Maria swore under her breath. She still wasn't looking at me.

Now. Do it.

In a single movement, I grabbed the knife and kicked out at her.

Caught off guard, she stumbled sideways. I kicked again.

'Aaagh!' Maria fell over the side of the boat and landed in the water with an awesome splash.

I jumped onto the landing board, the knife clutched between my fingers, and raced onto the beach.

'Run!' I yelled and headed for the trees.

The sand shifted under my feet as I reached the woodland to the left. I dived, panting, into the trees. Ketty and Ed raced up behind me.

I turned. Maria was stomping out of the sea, drenched and dripping.

'Come back, you little bastards,' she yelled.

'Stand still,' I ordered Ketty. 'Back to back.'

She stood, rigid, her back towards mine as I felt behind me for her wrists and positioned the knife against the plastic binding. I sliced upwards with the knife, praying I wasn't cutting into her hands. The binding gave way.

'Now do me.'

Ketty turned, took the knife and cut through the plastic round my own wrists. As she cut Ed free, I peered out from behind a tree. Maria was on the beach now but facing away from us, towards the boat.

'James?' she yelled. 'James! Get out here.'

'Let's go,' I whispered.

'What about Nico?' Ketty hissed. She and Ed were hiding behind the next tree along.

'We'll get help,' I said. 'Come back.'

'There isn't time. Look.' Ed pointed towards the boat. James was crossing the deck, half pushing, half dragging a stumbling Nico by the elbow.

Even from this distance it was obvious Nico had been

beaten. He was limping and one side of his face looked red and swollen.

'Oh, God,' Ketty gasped. She made a move towards the beach.

'Wait.' I said. 'Rushing out there's a real bad idea.'

Ketty hesitated, then nodded and stepped back behind her tree. As we watched, the rain grew stronger. It pattered onto the leaves all around us. Wet on our heads . . . our faces.

'They've got away, James, through there.' Maria pointed towards the trees where we were standing. 'We have to get them back . . . our cover will be blown if we don't take them to camp.'

James swore. Nico's head rose. He glanced round. James shoved him towards the wooden landing board. Nico jumped down. He winced as he landed, then walked on, his limp even more pronounced.

'What do we do?' Ed groaned.

'We can't leave him.' Ketty sounded desperate.

'Wait.' The rain was falling even harder now, drumming onto the trees above our heads. It was soaking through my top, making my back damp.

I glanced at the plastic that had tied Ketty's wrists. It was cut into two pieces now, but could still be tied in the normal way . . . the way I'd tied up James, before. I grabbed the other bindings off Ketty.

James and Nico were on the beach now. As James and Maria talked in low voices, the rain grew even stronger, soaking my hair and dripping down my neck. Normally when it rains I use my protective abilities to keep the wetness off my hair and neck. I hate it when my hair goes frizzy. But that was the last thing on my mind now.

James pushed Nico onto his knees and drew his gun out of his pocket.

I shrank against my tree. I hate guns. My aunt and uncle in Philadelphia taught us all to shoot, but I never liked doing it.

'Dylan?' James yelled towards the trees. 'Ed? Ketty? I know you're there.' He pressed the barrel of his gun against Nico's head. 'Come out, now!'

'Oh, *no*.' Ketty sort of crumpled against me.

I caught her arm.

'We have to go out there,' she said.

'Wait . . . he's bluffing . . .'

'But he's going to shoot Nico.' Ed was hopping up and down, his breath coming in short bursts. 'Oh God, oh God, oh God.'

'No,' I said. 'You heard Maria. They need us alive.'

'Hurry, or Nico's dead!' James yelled towards the trees. 'If you don't come back, I don't have anything to lose.'

I stared at him. Did he mean that? He certainly *looked* desperate enough to kill. So did Maria. She stood beside James, shivering, with her hair plastered to her head and her arms hugging her chest.

A drip of rain rolled down my forehead. Almost without

thinking, I focused on the force inside me that keeps any physical element away from my skin. The raindrop teetered on the end of my eyebrow, then fell away.

Of course.

'Storm,' I yelled. 'There needs to be a *storm*, Nico.'

'What are you doing?' Ketty hissed.

I kept my gaze on the beach. James and Maria were staring towards us. They exchanged a few words we couldn't hear, then Maria started walking in our direction.

Nico's head was turned towards us too. He was still bound and blindfolded. I hoped the blindfold was tied on tight.

'Storm, Nico,' I yelled again. 'Make a storm.'

'What are you talking about?' Ed gestured at the rain dripping off the leaves. 'There's already a storm. And you're giving away where we are.'

'Anyway, Nico can't control the weather,' Ketty added.

'Not rain, not rain . . .' I muttered, shoving all the plastic bindings into my pocket. 'Come *on*, Nico.'

Across the sand, Nico grinned, then kicked off his shoes.

'Yes!' I said. 'He understands. Stay here. Cover your eyes.'

'What?'

I grabbed the knife from Ketty's hands and stepped out from the trees. The sand around Nico whirled up into the air.

'More!' I yelled.

More sand flew into the air. Higher and higher – tornados of it . James and Maria turned away, covering their eyes, as the sand engulfed them. The swirling twisters spread across the beach. With his blindfold on, Nico's eyes would be protected, but he'd have no idea where to direct the sand. It whirled around me, forcing its way against my face and inside my clothes. Squinting, I concentrated all my energy into protecting the tiny space in front of my eyes, then charged forward into the heart of the sandstorm. James and Maria and Nico were just dark blurs now. I ran harder. Against the wind, against the rain, against the sand – only caring about the tiny space in front of my eyes. It took all of my focus to keep it clear.

I reached Maria first. She was bent over, the sunglasses gone, her palms pressed over her eyes. I grabbed her wrists and pulled one of the plastic bindings out of my pocket. I tied it as tightly as I could round her hands.

'No. Stop!' Maria flailed out at me, but her eyes were shut tight against the storm and it was easy to sidestep her bound hands.

I bent down, still keeping my focus on protecting my eyes, and tied her ankles with another length of plastic twine. *There*. I shoved her down onto the beach and stumbled through the raging sandstorm across to Nico.

'Keep it going,' I shouted above the roar.

Nico was standing now. I took the knife and held it so that the sharp blade was against his own wrist binding.

'Stay still.'

As I yelled out, my focus slid from my eyes and a shard of sand stung me. *Shit*. Trembling, I sliced upwards with the knife. The plastic binding gave way. Nico spun round, grabbed the knife. My energy was fading. Sand whipped around me, forcing its way against my scalp, inside my mouth. Tiny grains danced in front of my eyes. I looked round. Maria was still on the sand, curled up in a ball, as it beat against her. But where was James?

Nico tore the blindfold off. Sand swept towards his eyes. 'Aaagh.' He immediately directed the storm away from us, back towards Maria.

A roar. James lunged into view. He dragged Nico to the ground. The tornado blazed up again.The knife Nico had been holding fell onto the sand, then whirled out of reach.

James and Nico rolled on the sand, fighting. Nico closed his eyes. The sandstorm around them grew even bigger. Fiercer.

'Make it stop!' James yelled.

I could just make out his gun, waving dangerously in his hand above their heads. I grabbed it and threw it across the sand. At the same moment, Nico opened his eyes and reached out his palm. The knife which had fallen across the beach soared back towards him.

'You bastard,' Nico yelled. His eyes were bloodshot, his face sore and swollen. The knife flew into his hands. He held it there, poised over James's neck, his whole body trembling with fury.

'No.' I reached through the storm and put my hand on

Nico's shoulder. Sand was flickering right in front of my eyes now, each tiny particle threatening to pierce my eyeballs. 'That's enough.'

With a roar of frustration, Nico flicked his hand. The knife fell with a thud onto the sand beside James's head. I grabbed the plastic rope that had fallen from Nico's own wrists and wound it quickly round James's hands. I fastened it firmly, then tied his ankles, as Nico sat back with a sigh.

The sandstorm around us stopped. James and Maria knelt up, heads bowed, eyes red and raw.

'Undo us now,' James ordered.

'*Please*.' Maria was weeping.

Ignoring them, I glanced round. Nico was covered in sand from head to foot. I was too. The others rushed over. They both looked sandswept, though nowhere near as badly as we were. Ketty swung Nico round.

'Are you all right?' she cried. 'Oh, look at your face!'

'I'm fine, babe,' he said gruffly.

I pointed to James and Maria. 'Let's get these two onto the boat,' I said, picking up the knife.

'Sure.' Nico reached forward and grabbed the velvet bag of diamonds from James's pocket. He handed it to me.

'Move!' I ordered.

'Okay, okay,' James grunted.

Maria bowed her head.

A couple of minutes later they were locked in the cabin that Ed, Ketty and I had been trapped in earlier.

As we walked away, I smiled to myself. What was it Ketty had called us? Team Medusa.

We *were* a team.

I patted the velvet bag of diamonds.

'What now?' Ed asked.

'We need to find a phone,' Nico said.

'Here.' Ketty had been investigating the main cabin on the boat. She held out a canvas bag. 'All our mobiles are inside.'

I grabbed mine. No signal. None of the others had one, either.

'Come on,' Ketty said. 'Let's go along the beach. Head for one of those cottages.'

We left James and Maria locked up and raced along the beach. There were no cars on the dirt track that led up to the nearest set of small shops and houses, but a sign saying *internet access* swung from Bert's Café on the corner.

'Guess we're not in France, then,' Nico muttered.

As we burst into the café, the guy behind the counter looked horrified. Though we'd brushed our clothes down, we were all still covered in sand. Thanks to the rain it had stuck to our clothes like glitter make-up. We must have looked like total freaks. It had got underneath my clothes too. I could feel it covering my whole body like an itchy rash.

'A hot shower would be awesome right now,' I muttered.

'I know,' Ketty nodded.

'Please may we use the computer?' Ed asked.

The guy at the counter nodded, then pointed to a sign which demanded £2 as a minimum fee.

Ed dug his hands in his pocket and pulled out some coins and a pile of sand.

'Is there a phone here?' Nico asked.

'On the wall.'

Nico went off to call Geri Paterson while Ketty and I stood over Ed as he logged on. A couple of minutes later we were still standing there, mouths open, unable to believe what we were seeing.

'So it's true,' Ketty breathed. 'We no longer exist. All our records say we're dead.'

It was incredible. Every database or social networking site that Ed attempted to access either had no record of us – or said that we were no longer alive.

I turned to Nico, still hanging on the phone on the opposite wall. 'I can't get through,' he said.

'Come see this,' I called.

The door opened. I swung round. Geri Paterson, the head of the Medusa Project, stood in the doorway. She strode in, then stopped abruptly. Her blonde bob swung, as she flicked her gaze from me to Ed to Nico to Ketty.

'Oh my goodness,' she gasped. 'My *dears*.' She looked at me again. 'What happened?'

We went outside and told her everything, then Geri explained that she had found us by tracking and triangulating our mobiles.

'I got suspicious when the intelligence chatter we were following suggested Foster was nowhere near you last night.' She shook her head. 'James came with the highest recommendations. I can't believe he used you like this – and as for Maria . . .'

'I saw her looking at James like she really liked him a couple of times in the car,' Ketty said, thoughtfully.

I snorted. 'That's no freakin' excuse.'

'Quite,' Geri agreed. 'And it means we *still* don't know who Foster's spy is.' She made a call and two minutes later a couple of police cars whizzed past us down the dirt track.

The rain had stopped now. Geri, for once, was in loafers and jeans instead of her usual smart heels and pantsuit. She led us onto the beach, seemingly lost in her own thoughts.

I watched the waves crashing onto the sand and felt in my pocket for the bag of diamonds. For a second I contemplated making some excuse to be alone for a moment and taking one. They were *sooo* beautiful. But I knew I couldn't. It wasn't right.

And, anyway, someone would notice one was missing.

'Here.' I handed Geri the bag. 'These are the diamonds James made us steal.'

Geri sighed. 'We'll get them back to the Carters.'

'Could you find out if Mr Carter is okay?' Ed asked.

'Of course, dear,' Geri said. 'Right. I'm escorting you to your training camp personally now. It's going to be a different camp, of course. We don't know who James and Maria have been talking to and we can't risk anyone finding out where you are. But it'll give you a chance to rest . . . put an end to all the drama of the past few days.'

'Except . . . er . . . there's something else,' Ed said. 'James somehow managed to alter our records to make out we were dead.'

'Yeah,' I added. 'We were just looking on the internet. All our records say we no longer exist. Everywhere we looked.'

Geri cleared her throat. 'That wasn't James,' she said. 'That was me.'

I stared at her. '*What?*'

Nico looked at her, a blank expression on his face. 'Why make out we're dead? What's the point?'

'Your own protection, dear,' Geri said briskly. 'Foster knows of your existence. There are other undesirable elements that do as well. It puts you at risk . . . *and* Fox Academy *and* all its students. We have to cut your links with your old life. Completely.'

'Does that mean we're not going back to school after training camp?' Ketty asked.

'That's right, dear,' Geri said.

There was a silence as this sank in. A seagull squawked overhead.

'Why didn't you tell us before?' Nico demanded.

'What about our parents?' Ed's voice rose as he spoke. 'What have you said to them?'

There was a pause. Geri cleared her throat. 'They know you're alive, but not where we're taking you,' she said. 'It's for *their* protection too. Because of their connection with you, all your families are at risk.'

Nico's mouth fell open. I stared at the waves crashing onto the beach.

'So when can we see them . . . speak to them?' Ketty asked.

'Are you saying we have to wait the whole two months we'll be in the training camp?' Nico demanded.

'Longer,' Geri said. 'We need to let the situation settle first, make sure no one knows where you are . . . that you're safe.' She paused. 'You'll be in the training camp with no access to your family for at least six months. As far as everyone else is concerned, you died last night.'

'*What!*' Nico and I exploded together.

'*No.*' Ed's face blanched. 'No – you can't do this. I need to speak to my parents.'

'I'm sorry, dear, but it's done,' Geri said. 'It's a shame you had to find out like this. I was going to tell you once you reached camp. But it is for the best.'

I glanced at Ed and Ketty. They both looked close to tears. Nico put his arms round Ketty and she hugged him back.

I turned away, feeling all mixed up. I guess I didn't care if I never saw my aunt and uncle and my cousins Paige and Tod again – but having my identity stolen away like this was horrible. I couldn't imagine how the others must be feeling.

Behind me, I heard Nico speak. 'So, Geri,' – his voice was hard and angry – 'you're the *real* thief.'

I caught Ketty's eye, remembering her earlier vision of Nico saying exactly that.

'You've stolen our *lives*,' Nico went on. 'James might have got us to steal some diamonds, but if you hadn't sent us after criminals like Foster, none of them would even know we existed and we wouldn't *need* to spend time in hiding.'

Geri sighed. 'You're all overwrought, and it's not surprising. Let's get the car. There's a hotel we can stop at for a shower and a change of clothes. I'm still finalising the details of the new camp we're sending you to. We'll talk more later.'

She strode off across the damp sand, leaving the four of us standing in silence. A tear trickled down Ketty's cheek.

'We'll be okay,' I said. 'Never mind everyone thinking we're freakin' dead. We can look after ourselves.'

Ketty stared at me.

'And each other,' Nico said, putting his arm round her.

'Yeah . . . *and* each other.' I looked from Ketty to Ed.

He shrugged, then attempted a shy smile. I grinned back at him – at all of them.

'Boot camp, then,' I said. 'Bring it on.'

THE ADVENTURE CONTINUES IN . . .
THE RESCUE, COMING SOON.

WIN!

To celebrate World Book Day 2010, one lucky winner will have the opportunity to WIN an iPod Touch 8GB preloaded with Nico, Ketty, Dylan and Ed's playlists plus £50 worth of itunes vouchers.

To be in with a chance to win this state of the art prize and be the envy of all your friends visit:

www.themedusaproject.co.uk

Don't forget to check out the other titles in *The Medusa Project* series

Competition Terms & Conditions:
This competition will run from 28th February until midnight on 2nd April 2010. The promoter of this competition is Simon and Schuster UK, 1st Floor, 222 Gray's Inn Road, London, WC1X 8HB. The competition is open to residents of the United Kingdom only, excluding employees or agents of Simon and Schuster UK or anyone else connected to the competition and/or their immediate family. Only entries made online via the Internet will be accepted. No purchase is necessary to enter this competition. Simon and Schuster UK does not accept responsibility for lost, damaged or illegal entries. 1 winner will be selected; at random from the correct entries. The winners will be selected by 9th April 2010. The judges' decision is final. No cash alternative is available for any prize. For a full list of terms and conditions please visit www.themedusaproject.co.uk

You don't need psychic powers
to conjure up another fantastic story...

FLIP OVER FOR ANOTHER RIVETING READ!

Visit
www.sophiemckenziebooks.com
to read an extract from Sophie's next
exciting Medusa Project adventure:
THE RESCUE – publishing in July!

WALKING THE WALLS

This book has been specially written and published for World Book Day 2010. World Book Day is a worldwide celebration of books and reading, with events held last year in countries as far apart as Afghanistan and Australia, Nigeria and Uruguay. For further information please see www.worldbookday.com

World Book Day in the UK and Ireland is made possible by generous sponsorship from National Book Tokens, participating publishers, authors and booksellers. Booksellers who accept the £1 World Book Day Token kindly agree to bear the full cost of redeeming it.

Also by Chris Higgins

32C That's Me
Pride and Penalties
It's a 50/50 Thing
A Perfect 10
Love Ya Babe
Would You Rather?
Tapas and Tears

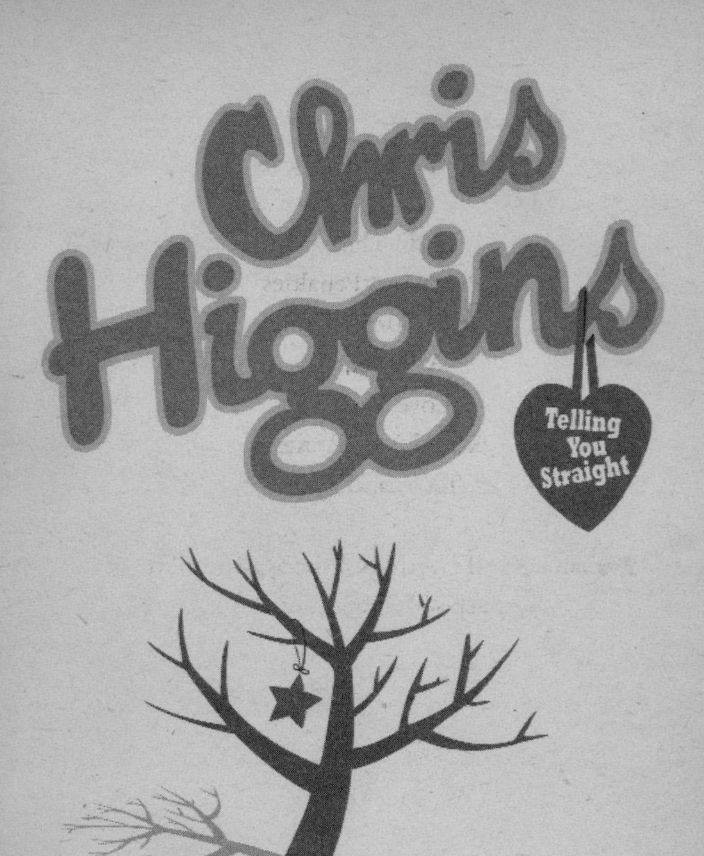

WALKING THE WALLS

Hodder Children's Books
A division of Hachette Children's Books

For Vinny, Zac and Ella

This World Book Day book published in Great Britain by
Hodder Children's Books/Simon and Schuster UK Ltd in 2010

1

A Catalogue record for this book is available from the British Library

ISBN 978 0 956 28778 6

Typeset in Bembo by Avon DataSet Ltd,
Bidford on Avon, Warwickshire

Printed and bound in Great Britain by
CPI Bookmarque, Croydon, CR0 4TD

The text paper within this book was donated by Abitibi Consolidated and Paper Management Services Ltd

The paper and board used in this paperback by Hodder Children's Books are natural recyclable products made from wood grown in sustainable forests. The manufacturing processes conform to the environmental regulations of the country of origin.

Hodder Children's Books
www.hodderchildrens.co.uk
a division of Hachette Children's Books
338 Euston Road, London NW1 3BH
An Hachette UK company
www.hachette.co.uk

First day back of the school year and I notice the kid straight away, lining up outside the hall for the new intake assembly. You can't miss him with that bright ginger hair and the skin that goes with it, splattered with freckles. He stands out amongst the colony of indistinguishable grey seals shuffling in a line up the corridor, with his red tufted hair and the splotchy brown blotches on his face, like a pup that hasn't quite lost his baby camouflage.

Only it doesn't conceal him, that's the trouble. Even in the regulation gun-metal-coloured uniform, his brand-new blazer reaching practically to his knees, he's already a marked man. And he knows it. It's not just his hair that grabs my attention: it's his quiet watchfulness, head down but eyes darting quickly from side to side like he knows he's got to be permanently on guard in case of attack.

I understand what that feels like.

A thud and my knee suddenly gives way beneath me. I stumble forward into a screech of Year 9 girls, my bag falling from my shoulder. They turn to glare at me, then their faces break into smiles.

'Hiya, Felix! How you doing?'

Girls like me. Boys don't. Not the kind of sad, fascist,

homophobic losers who go round in gangs and are afraid to have a single original thought in their heads, anyway. Like the ugly, slime-producing gastropod sneering at me when I turn around to see who gave me a dead leg this time. It's Slug. Simon Lugg, from my class. I've got complacent in the school holidays. I'd forgotten about him and his mean little ways.

'Sorry, Felix. Didn't mean to kick you. Thought you were the cat!'

Old joke but it makes his sidekicks crease up.

'Get lost, Molluscs!' I say, which makes them laugh even more as they disappear down the corridor. They always laugh if they don't understand something, so basically they bust a gut all through the school day, tittering at teachers, jeering through geography, mocking maths, sending up science, falling about in French, arseing their way through art. I find *that* particularly annoying because art is my favourite subject.

Beside me the new Year 7s shift uneasily in the queue. I don't blame them. They've probably heard all the stories I heard about the Sec before I started here: how they stick the new boys' heads down the toilets; how they take their trousers off and hide them; how they force them to eat disgusting stuff and lick the bottoms of their shoes.

None of this is true by the way. If it was, it would've happened to me.

That doesn't mean no bullying goes on. It does. But not that much of it is physical, to be fair. Only thickos like Slug and his slimy trail of followers resort to that

occasionally. Most of the time people use psychology: ostracization and verbal intimidation being the favourites. Even that's not very subtle. Just offensive. I've been called it all in my time.

Pretty boy! Weirdo! Freak! Geek! Nerd!

And much worse. Believe me.

'Never mind, Fee! Sticks and stones may break your bones but names can never hurt you.'

That's what Gabby drilled into me before I started the Sec. It works on the whole.

'It's only words. Tell me and Angie if anyone picks on you and we'll sort them out.'

My older sister Gabby is fearless. She had her own problems to deal with when she started school, from this gang of girls known as the Gemstones. They leant on her in a girly way, coming in between her and her best friend Angie, spreading rumours around that she'd been with Angie's boyfriend, that she was pregnant by him! It was all lies. They even tried to make her shoplift for them. Personally, I think that's worse than getting a dead leg once in a while. But the difference was, Gabby had a best mate to stick up for her.

I wish I had a best mate.

'You'll make friends when you get to secondary school, Fee, like I did,' said Gabby.

I did make friends. Eventually. Just not close friends. It's like some boys were afraid of being seen to be too close to me in case they got tagged 'pretty boy' or 'geek' too.

Angie says my problem is I'm just too good-looking for

my own good. Plus I'm bright. Not the best combination to survive the Sec.

Anyway, at least I had my sister and her mate to look out for me.

Gabby and Angie took their GCSEs this summer. They both did really well. Now they've stayed on in the Sixth Form to do A levels so they can get in to uni.

The Gemstones didn't do well in their exams. They've all left school.

Slug and his snails won't be around for ever. Sticks and stones. Slugs and snails. I can cope with them all nowadays.

I pick my bag up off the floor and stick it back on my shoulder. As I do, the ginger kid's eyes dart to mine. I give him a wink. A ghost of a smile hovers for a second on his lips before he looks away.

Poor kid. I'd hate to be starting again in Year 7.

One good thing about being in Year 9 at our school is that they give you a bit of choice so you can select the subjects you like and drop the ones you hate. Well, not all of them. You have to do some subjects, like English, maths and science, whether you like them or not, because they're part of the National Curriculum. I'm not sure who decides this. If I was in charge I would definitely make music, art and English compulsory and maths, science and games optional. Or better still, I'd ban them altogether.

I think the same sadist who drew up the National Curriculum also thought up the standard method for choosing teams used by every school in the country. It goes something like this. The sports teacher, usually a screwball himself, picks the two biggest and most competitive psychos in the year as opposing captains then sits back smugly while they select their teams one by one. This ensures without fail that the nutters are dispersed and that I will be left at the end as the one person nobody wants on their team. By default this makes me feel the least popular person in the year. Apparently, according to my father who is uncommonly in touch with his feelings nowadays having being made redundant from

his high-powered city job during the recession, you never get over this.

I think he's feeling a bit rejected himself at the moment, which has probably brought it all back.

Another thing about being in Year 9 is that they set you in ability groups instead of teaching you all together in one massive melting pot. Some people, including my father, himself a product of the private school system, think this should work, because you get like-minded people working together. Or to put it more bluntly, you get all the geeks together in the top group (Talented and Gifted . . . TAGS . . . we do like our labels, don't we?), the ordinary kids in the middle groups, and all the thickos and headbangers hidden away in the bottom group to be taken out on a quickly arranged day trip when the Ofsted inspectors come.

Doesn't work though. Because my favourite subject is art. And art is timetabled against a second language, which I wouldn't mind taking if I could, but then I couldn't draw and if I can't draw, I might as well not breathe. So, against Dad's wishes, I signed up for art last July which now means I'm sitting in the art room with 29 of Year 9's most brain-dead morons at one end of the spectrum and certifiable psychopaths at the other.

And they think *I'm* the fruitcake.

'This term we're going to have fun,' announces Jacko doubtfully, eyeing his new art class, nearly all boys. Mr Jackson is a good guy and creditable artist, but somewhat lacking in classroom control. My heart sinks. I hate that

word fun. It always means chaos. 'It's all about identity. We're going to find out about ourselves and get to know each other.' My heart sinks even further.

'We know each other already, sir,' says Graham Slick. 'Jed's a nutter, Gav's a nob-head and Felix is a fairy!'

Slug bellows like a cow giving birth and everyone else but me titters obediently, even Jed Saunders who looks quite flattered to be called a nutter and Gavin Pritchard who wouldn't object to anything Graham Slick decides to call him, just so long as he leaves him well alone.

Jacko glances around nervously and says, 'Listen up now all of you, listen up.' Where do teachers get these phrases from? Do they go home and say to their wives, 'Listen up!' Or when their front doorbell rings do they roar, 'Sit down! That bell is a signal for me and not for you!' And if they're standing in the queue at Tesco, do they fold their arms and tap their foot and say smugly to all and sundry, 'It doesn't matter to me! It's not my time you're wasting!'

Anyway, I digress. (Another favourite of teachers!) 'We're going to do collage,' Jacko announces and, predictably, a universal groan echoes round the room. Actually, I'm with them on this one, though I know they would've groaned whatever he'd said. Unless of course, he'd announced, 'We're going to do life-drawing today and a page three model is going to pose for us.'

I wish we were doing life-drawing.

'We're all going to make a collage of ourselves,' Jacko battles on manfully, even though actually this is a lie. Teachers always say 'We' even though they never do

anything themselves other than yell at us to get on with it. 'I want you to brainstorm your favourite things.' He doles out big pieces of lining paper and a felt-tip to each person in the room. Wise move, Jacko, stalling the normal 'Can't, sir, haven't got a pen' objections. 'Now then, write down the things that are important to you.'

'Sex!' leers Slug, writing it in big block capitals across his page. He even manages to spell it properly. I'm impressed.

'Put down your favourite book,' Jacko continues, striving to ignore him. Twenty-nine faces stare at him incredulously. 'Or your favourite fruit,' he adds quickly.

'Don't like fruit,' says Jed morosely.

'You're supposed to have it five times a day,' says Jacko, trying to jolly him along.

'What? Sex?' yells Slug and everyone falls about laughing.

'In your dreams,' I say under my breath and start doodling clouds on my paper. Slug gives me a suspicious look.

'Think of your favourite animal . . .'

'Baa . . .' bleats Slick then says, 'Oh sorry, that's Felix's.'

'Sheep-shagger!' chortles Slug who's caught his drift. The class roars appreciatively. There's no logic to this. How can I be a fairy *and* a sheep-shagger? I add legs to a cloud and turn it into a sheep then do the same to the others.

'Now think of your favourite activity.' Jacko moves on hurriedly.

There's a tirade of obscenities as most of the boys in the class compete to describe their preferred methods of

entertainment. I never would've thought they could be so imaginative. 'Don't discuss them. Write them down!' instructs Jacko, a bit unnerved. I sketch a boy lying in a hammock slung between two trees. He's got earphones on and he's listening to music and drawing.

The class settles down and starts writing. 'Best film! Best music! Best TV programme!' Jacko's on a roll, now he's finally got everyone's attention. I draw a saxophone.

'Who's your hero? The person you look up to most?' A noisy discussion breaks out about sporting, music and movie celebs and random people who've shot to fame through YouTube. I make an outline drawing of Charlie Chaplin, unmistakable in his trademark bowler hat, walking stick, baggy trousers and toothbrush moustache, looking a bit lost.

Brave little guy. I've seen all his films. Him against the world.

'You're good.'

I look up. Behind me a girl is examining the doodles on my page. I noticed her when I came in, painting at the back of the art room. She's one of the Year 10s who are allowed in any time to work on their coursework. I've spotted her before around the school. She's kind of funky even in boring school uniform because she's got a row of tiny studs in her left ear and a headband to keep her spiky purple fringe out of her eyes. She's also wearing a man's shirt that is far too big for her. She looks cool. I always notice what people are wearing because I want to be a designer when I grow up.

No other girl in this school would wear a man's shirt.

And still manage to look sort of soft and floaty at the same time.

'Really good,' she repeats.

'Thanks.'

'I love bowler hats,' she says, looking at Charlie. 'I've been trying to get one everywhere.'

'There's one in the window of the Cancer Research Shop in town.'

'Is there!' Her eyes sparkle. 'I'm going to get it!'

'You've got paint on your nose.'

She wrinkles it up and scrubs at it with the palm of her hand. Too late I realize it's a spattering of tiny freckles so symmetric they look like drops of paint. How cute is that?

'Gone?'

'Yep,' I lie, glad they're still there.

'You're Felix, aren't you?'

'How do you know that?'

'Everyone knows you,' she says, but in a nice way.

Sort of flirty.

'Right then!' bawls Jacko. 'Listen up! Now you've made a list of things that are important to you, I want you to create a picture of yourself. Think of fun ways to represent these things.' People stare at him blankly. 'Like you, Jed,' he says valiantly, picking up his paper. 'You're a rugby fan. Maybe you could draw your head in the shape of a rugby ball . . .'

'What?' Jed looks confused. Loud jeers drown out the rest of Jacko's words. Jed's face darkens. 'I ain't got an 'ead like no rugby ball!' he protests. The class erupts.

'Time to go,' the girl whispers to me with a grin and drifts away.

Jacko should've quit while he was ahead. He's lost it now. Jed, certain he's been insulted, gets up, kicks his chair over and tears up his paper. Slug leans over, scrunches mine up, and lobs it at Graham Slick. Soon balls of screwed-up paper and felt-tip pens are flying around the art room.

I watch as the girl packs up her stuff and leaves. I wish I could go with her.

Too late, I realize I don't even know her name.

I let myself into the house feeling fed up. I thought maybe things would be different in Year 9 but now I'm not so sure. First day back and I'm still the butt of the weirdo jokes. Listening to them, that girl must have thought I'm some kind of pervert.

Freddie, my nine-year-old brother, is lying on the couch, munching chocolate biscuits out of a packet and watching CBeebies. When he sees me he crams the last two into his mouth. 'All gone,' he says triumphantly as biscuit crumbs spray from his mouth. Greedy pig!

My other brother, two-and-a-half-year-old Henry, who actually should be watching CBeebies, is playing on the floor with his dinosaurs. I squat down beside him.

'Hello, Mr Dinosaur,' I say, holding one aloft. Henry's face lights up and he picks up the other.

'Hello,' says his dinosaur back.

'Have you had a nice day?' asks my dinosaur.

'Yes.' Pause while Henry sifts through his memory. 'Beans,' says his dinosaur. 'Café.'

'Nice.' Henry's idea of a perfect day. Baked beans on toast for lunch in BHS cafeteria. 'What else did you do?'

Henry's dinosaur struggles but he can't remember.

'Cuddle?' he offers.

'Yes please.' The two dinosaurs have a cuddle.

'Bye,' says Henry's dinosaur. 'Love you. See you soon.'

'Love you,' mine replies, but it's too late, Henry's dinosaur is already discarded on the floor as his owner goes off to check on his mum.

I sit back on my haunches, feeling better already. If you're a bit down, have a cuddle with a dinosaur. Through the open door I can see Mum on the computer in Dad's study. She's writing her blog. Beside her, Henry sits down to investigate the contents of the waste-paper bin.

My two brothers are polar opposites. Freddie is a spoilt brat, the indulged baby of the family for almost seven years until Henry our surprise package arrived. Not a surprise to Mum, just to the rest of us. It turned out she'd planned it all along which didn't go down well with the rest of the family at all, except for me. I never minded having another baby brother, which is quite surprising when you think what a pain Freddie was. Is. But Gabby found it really embarrassing because Mum and Dad are quite a bit older than the average parents, and to be honest I think she was a bit surprised they were still doing it.

Poor old Henry, it wasn't his fault.

He was different from Freddie from the word go. Mind you, we're all different in our family, who am I to talk? 'That's because I had children, not sausages,' Mum says proudly.

Henry came in a bit of a rush. Mum nearly had him in Tesco in fact. It was a shame she didn't because apparently

she would've had free food for a year . . . I think . . . or maybe I'm just making that up. It was all a bit of a blur at the time because she ended up in hospital for ages with something called pre-eclampsia and she was really ill. Then when she came home she couldn't bond with the baby and she went a bit funny so Gabby and I had to look after him. So we've kind of brought Henry up between us.

I mean, Mum's in charge technically but she spends most of her time on her blog. Its called 'Confessions of a menopausal, aged-multiple, postnatal-depressive mother', and she writes about her day, which is quite hard if you think about it because all she does is blog.

'What has she got to blog about?' She doesn't *do* anything!' Gabby says. She gets really cross with Mum sometimes because she'll write about us. If she's not blogging, she's tweeting.

So the upshot of this is, Henry doesn't get that much attention. He doesn't seem to mind though, he's used to being ignored.

Conversely, Freddie, who was totally babied by Mum for the first seven years of his life until Henry and postnatal depression came along and Mum discovered the solace of the internet, can't bear not to be noticed.

Me, I'm with Henry on this. I think being the centre of attention is overrated. But the weird thing is, I always seem to attract more than my fair share of it.

The front door opens and Gabby blows in with Angie. Henry hears her from the study and comes charging through to rugby tackle her round the knees. Gabby

swings him upside down and he chuckles appreciatively.

'Hi, gorgeous!' trills Angie and tickles him in the ribs. Then she sees me and repeats, 'Hi, gorgeous!'

If anyone is gorgeous it's Angie. She's Jamaican with beautiful dark skin and huge brown eyes. Most of the boys in my year are lusting after her but to me it would be like lusting after my sister, I know her too well. That doesn't mean that I can't appreciate how lovely she is though. Not just her looks either. I owe a lot to Angie. She and Gabby kept an eye on me when I started at the Sec, and waded in if the going got tough. They knew I'd be a target.

Some people just seem to attract it.

Like that kid today.

'Staying for supper?' Mum breezes out of the study. Angie looks wildly at us for help. 'Good grief, is that the time? I don't know where the hours go.'

'How's your blog?' asks Gabby sweetly.

'Coming along nicely. See to Henry, will you, Gabby, while I get some food on? Your father will be home soon. Now then, how does mushroom risotto sound?'

Mushroom risotto sounds OK, but . . . my mother's cooking is infamous. She used to be organic, wholefood and vegetarian but nowadays, being a blogger and mother of four, she hasn't got time to spend on planning meals so she tends to pluck a dish out of her head and then try to assemble the ingredients at random from whatever she can lay her hands on. It's a bit hit and miss. In the end, out-of-date-tin-of-sardines-and-packet-of-frozen-peas risotto is what we actually sit down to.

I blame counselling. When Mum went funny after having Henry she had counselling from a woman called Marjorie who basically told her to stop putting everyone else first and find time for herself. Mum took Marjorie's advice literally and now she's so busy with 'Me-time' she hasn't got much left over for the rest of us.

Not that I think women should be tied to the kitchen sink. All of us are quite good at fending for ourselves (thanks to Marjorie), including Freddie who is ace at filling up on packets of biscuits and Henry who has got into the habit of helping himself to handfuls of cereal from the cupboard if Mum's a bit busy writing and has temporarily forgotten his existence. You can always tell if

Mum's blog is going well by the trail of Coco Pops between the kitchen and the telly.

But she does like us all to 'sit down together at the table as a family' in the evenings so we can 'talk about our day over a home-cooked meal'. And if you're not careful, like Angie, visitors get roped in as well, though most don't make the same mistake twice. Angie is just too nice for her own good.

'How was your day, Leonard?' asks Mum predictably as we all sit down.

'Fine,' says Dad as usual, eyeing his risotto with suspicion. He's always home for dinner now he's no longer a city analyst. He was made redundant just before Henry was born and now he helps out as a guide at a nearby stately home, which Gabby thinks is incredibly boring but I think is quite cool because they've got some amazing eighteenth-century costumes there, though I suppose even they could get a bit boring after a while. I think he likes it though because he's not half as bad-tempered as he used to be. He was always having a go at me about being a sissy, which was a tad unfair because I was never a crybaby, I just wasn't the son he wanted. I was useless at football and rugby and I would never stand up for myself, unlike Freddie who's ace at footie and is forever getting into fights.

Gabby, who can be quite perceptive, says she thinks he was a bit of a wimp when he was at school and was probably picked on and he doesn't want the same for me. Maybe she's right. He used to go mad when I dressed up in Gabby's clothes, which were always more interesting than

mine. He probably thought he'd got a tranny for a son.

That's what some of the boys call me at school. In some ways Dad's like them. He doesn't like it because I'm a bit unconventional, so he tries to make me conform.

'How was your day, Felix?'

'All right.'

'Gabby?'

'Why? Are you going to blog about it?' asks Gabby suspiciously.

'No darling, I'm just interested, that's all,' says Mum earnestly.

Reassured, my sister launches into a lengthy and convoluted explanation of her new Year 12 experience, assisted by Angie. I switch off, something I'm very good at. Girls are so verbal! I sometimes think Gabby does not possess a single thought in her head that she does not share with all and sundry by tongue, text or telephone. My mother's the same with her constant blogging. What is it with women? Like, who needs to know exactly what you're thinking 24/7?

Still, I prefer girls to boys. I don't think Dad's ever got that. I'm sure he's convinced I'm gay, though he'd never ask me straight out. I'm not, I like girls. I don't mean the giggly clones who pile on the lip-gloss and are the colour of satsumas! I mean the normal ones. They're less likely than boys to hang round in packs and they don't take the mickey out of each other all the time. I especially like girls who are not scared to be different.

Like that girl in the art room.

After supper I offer to carry Angie's books home for her. No really, I do! She's borrowed loads from us, as usual, and they're heavy. Dad's got shelves full of classics in his study and Angie's reading her way through them now she's doing A-level English. She reckons we're better than the public library.

We walk across the common to the flats where Angie lives, chatting away. I'm taller than her now; Mum's right, I've shot up this year. In assembly this morning I noticed I was one of the tallest people in the year. Mind you, I'm one of the oldest too. Sometimes I think that's why I find most of the boys in my year so childish.

We're so busy chatting I take no notice of the gang kicking a ball around until I hear a shout, then someone calling my name in a high, mocking way.

'Fee-lix!'

'Someone's calling you,' says Angie. I glance over without stopping and spot Slug's sneering face.

'Ignore them,' I say. 'They're just taking the piss.'

Sure enough, the catcalls start coming.

'Fee-lix! What's with the girl?'

'Yeah. Where's your boyfriend tonight?'

'Felix is a poofter.'

They all join in like a chorus. '*Felix is a poofter* . . .' followed by raucous laughter.

Angie's face darkens. 'Put down those books and push me up against that tree!' she says suddenly, out of the corner of her mouth.

'What?'

'Do as I say. Now!'

I let the books fall to the ground and push her hard against a big sycamore. 'Now kiss me!' she says under her breath.

'Angie!'

'Just do it!'

I do as I'm told. As I move towards her, her arms go round my neck and she pulls me in to her. I can feel her boobs surprisingly soft and squashy against my chest and her hair smells nice. My lips meet hers in a chaste, brotherly kiss but she grabs me harder and gives me a full-on snog. I gasp in surprise and pull away but she hisses, 'Make out you're enjoying it!' and goes in again. Behind me Slug and his gang fall silent.

At last Angie surfaces, winks at me, then turns to her gobsmacked audience. 'Are you still here?' she asks, feigning surprise. 'Run along, boys, it's past your bedtime!'

Slug's face is a picture.

I pick up Angie's books. She wraps her arm round my waist, leans her head on my shoulder and we walk off together across the common, trying not to laugh.

'Put your arm round me!' orders Angie. 'They're still watching.'

Coming towards us along the path is a girl. Not just any

girl. She's wearing a bowler hat and an oversized man's shirt over her school skirt. She's walking with her head down, in a world of her own.

'Hi!' I say as we pass.

She looks up startled. Her eyes flick from me to Angie and back again. Too late, I realize we're still wrapped round each other. 'Hi!' she says.

'Keep walking,' warns Angie. I do as I'm told, not having much choice really, seeing as Angie's marching me along in a vice-like grip. When we've gone round the corner out of sight, she lets go and dissolves into laughter.

'Sorry, Fee, I know that was weird, but I had to do something. Little shits!'

'I don't mind! I think you've just made my street-cred go through the roof.'

'Hope so.' She giggles. 'Did you see their faces?'

Angie's big brown eyes are shining with laughter. She is so gorgeous with her smooth, dusky skin, high cheekbones and white, even teeth, she could be a model.

Most boys in my year would rip their right arm off to snog her.

Most boys in my year would rip their right arm off to snog any Year 12 girl.

Most boys in my year would rip their right arm off to snog any girl, full stop.

And I got the prize. My first kiss and I get to snog Angie.

She was right though, it *was* weird. I know her too well. It was like snogging my sister.

Don't go there.

I keep seeing that ginger kid around the school, almost every day.

I see him lining up with his class outside the maths room, which is opposite mine, waiting for the teacher to turn up and let them in. He's usually one of the first to arrive but he's always one of the last to go in. He ends up at the back of the queue as kids turn up and push in next to their mates. They don't notice him as he shuffles back accommodatingly to let them in.

I see him in the canteen at lunchtime. He's either sitting on his own or he's perched at the end of a crowded table as if he's got no right to be there. Sometimes I see him trying to engage someone in conversation and it works for a while but then they move on and he's left on his own again.

I see him walking the walls. You'd have to have done this yourself to understand what I mean by this.

You see, most of the intimidation in schools takes place during break and lunchtime. And our school has an open door policy. Unlike most schools, our liberal head, Mr Roberts, who hasn't got a clue, thinks that civilized children shouldn't be slung outside at break or lunchtime,

they should have access to their classrooms. The trouble is not all the kids in our school are civilized. The staff hate it because they say this is when all the trouble breaks out and damage occurs. They're right.

But they just see the damage done to their classrooms, not the damage done to kids, because that's not normally visible except for the comparatively few times proper fights break out. That doesn't mean things don't happen though. Teasing, baiting, name-calling, threats – they're all pretty run of the mill. So are punching, hair-pulling, finger twisting and Chinese burns, not to mention ignoring, excluding, whispering, spreading rumours and ganging up. Then there's writing on boards, abusive text messages, nicking stuff, destroying property . . . Need I go on?

It may sound horrific but it's all in the name of 'Just having a laugh, sir!' if any teacher pops his head round the door between the hours of one and two to see what's going on. And I'm telling you for real, if you're the poor sod who's the butt of any of these comedy routines, the last thing you are going to say is, 'Actually, sir, it's not funny.'

No wonder the kid prefers to walk the walls.

I see him stalking the corridors, head down, looking purposeful, his bag slung over his shoulder. He keeps to the outside edge away from classroom doors, just like I did. It takes twelve minutes and thirty-nine seconds exactly to walk round each floor of the school. I remember it well.

How did it go?

Eat your lunch slowly, go to the toilet, walk the

walls. Go up to the first floor, put your head in the IT room, pretend you're looking for someone. Walk the walls. Slow down a bit. Go up to the next floor, put your head in the library, pretend you're looking for someone. Walk the walls. If you're lucky you may bump into your sister or some of her mates and you can get into conversation for a bit. Go back down to the ground floor, go to the toilet again (don't linger this time, lots of people in there now!) and then, with luck, you've used up nearly the whole of lunchtime without getting picked on or making it too obvious you haven't got a friend to spend it with.

Today he hasn't timed it right though. When I come across him he's on his knees picking up the contents of his bag which have been strewn across the floor. Two Year 7s tear off down the corridor when they see me. I bend down to give him a hand.

'You OK?'

'Yeah.'

He won't look at me. He's embarrassed.

'They're giving you a hard time?'

'No.' His face is closed and he's clammed up like a mute. I gather up his pencil case, his calculator, his books, all of them labelled in a tiny neat script, and hand them back to him. He takes them without a word and stuffs them into his bag but not before I notice his first name has been scrawled out on his exercise books and rewritten in big untidy letters.

I can't see what his real name is but I can see what they've rechristened him.

Carrot.

Not very original.

Not very funny.

Hurts though.

'It's not your fault,' I say.

He turns away and walks off down the corridor without a word.

I've made it sound like I'm some kind of basket case with no mates whatsoever. It's not true. There are guys in my year I get along with and by the end of Year 7 I'd discovered them. There's Sean and Logan and Deepak and Rhys for instance, all of them pretty sound people. But the thing is, we're not all in the same classes, plus we've all got other stuff going on. Like, Logan is a really good musician so he spends his spare time practising in the music room and Deepak and Rhys are computer boffs so they're always in the IT rooms, while Sean's got some medical condition and has to have physio every lunchtime to clear his lungs.

So even though snogging Angie has given me quite a bit of credibility around the school, I'm still at a loose end sometimes even in Year 9. Though hey, let's put this in perspective, I'd rather be hanging around at lunchtime with nothing to do than have my chest pummelled till I've coughed up wads of gunge like Sean. I mean, everything's relative.

One day, I'm bored out of my skull listening to the girls debating who's hot and who's grot (though it is gratifying to hear that Slug and Slick are officially losers), so I wander

along to the art room. Jacko's there, eating his sandwiches.

'Can I work on my collage, sir?'

He waves me in, mid-munch, and carries on reading his paper. A few Upper School students are in there too, working away. One of them is the girl. My heart leaps, but she keeps her head down, engrossed in her painting, oblivious to my presence. I don't like to interrupt her so I wander over to the Year 9 cupboard and pull out my folder and decide to start again. I mean, pictures of sheep to sum up my interests is just asking for trouble.

Soon I'm busy compiling a mind map of people and things that matter to me: Henry, Gabby, Angie . . . drawing, fashion, designing clothes . . . All the time I'm aware of the girl at the back of the art room. I'm dying to see what she's painting but when I turn around to peep at her, she's totally focused and I don't like to interrupt. I add 'Girl with purple hair' to my list.

Then suddenly she's there beside me, washing out her brushes at the sink, and I say, 'Hi!' and she turns around. Her eyes sweep over me, devoid of interest.

'Hi,' she says flatly and walks off.

I stare at her in surprise as she leaves the art room. Today she is wearing a man's waistcoat over her shirt – definitely not school uniform – long stripy socks and clumpy walking boots and she's tied her fringe up on top of her head in a big floppy bow with her school tie. I don't know how she manages it but she's the coolest-looking girl I've ever seen.

And she's blown me out.

The bell goes and I shove my folder in the cupboard and make my way gloomily back to my form room for afternoon registration.

My Year 9 form room, where from right down the end of the corridor I can hear pandemonium breaking out.

Get real, Felix. That girl is Year 10 and she's beautiful. Why did you ever think she'd be interested in you?

'How do you know if you're in love?' I ask Gabby.

She rests her chin on her hand and sighs deeply. 'You think about them all the time, day and night. So much, it hurts. And everywhere you go, you think you see them. Or someone who reminds you of them. You can't talk about anything else but them. You can't eat, you can't concentrate, you can't sleep. And if you do, you dream about them.'

Right. OK. Maybe I'm not in love then. My appetite is as huge as ever, I'm always starving hungry, and Mum says I can sleep for England.

'That's what love is like,' continues Gabby. 'Overwhelming, all-consuming, unrelenting, inexorable.'

I'm not sure what inexorable means but she must be right. Gabby is an authority on affairs of the heart. She's been in love loads of times. Once she and Angie fell out big time over a creep called Si who played them off one against the other. He was their first love. Or their first lust.

But she's right about one thing. I can't stop thinking about the girl with purple hair. And I see her everywhere. Literally. In the corridors, in the canteen, in the art room. Especially in the art room. The more I see her, the more I

want to be with her, but it's doing my head in because she always blanks me. Yet she was so friendly the first time she spoke to me, she really was, I know I'm not imagining it.

'Why are you asking?' asks Gabby. She's getting ready to go out on a date herself and I'm lying on her bed watching her. 'Black or brown?' She holds up two belts, one in each hand.

'Neither. Red's much better with what you've got on.'

'Yeah, you're right. As usual.' She ties a belt around her waist, musses up her hair and pouts at herself in the mirror. 'That'll do. Right then, Fee, what's all this about? Have you got a crush on someone?'

'I think so.'

I've always been pretty open with Gabby. She's been my ally against Dad all my life, sticking up for me when I fell short of being the macho son he wanted.

'Who is it?'

I pause, not wanting to say, well, actually, I don't know her name.

'Oh, my life!' Her eyes look like they're protruding from her head on wires. 'It's not Angie, is it?'

'NO WAY!'

'Are you sure? She told me she snogged you.'

'No! Definitely not!'

Gabby pipes down, convinced by my tone of voice, but continues to study me, her hands on her hips, brain going into overdrive. Suddenly she flops down on the bed beside me and grabs my hand in both of hers and stares at me intensely.

'What?'

'Is it a boy?' Her voice is soft and understanding.

'NO!!!' I shake her hands off in surprise, not knowing whether to laugh or be indignant. 'Gabby, you're as bad as Dad.'

'No I'm not!' she says but she looks relieved. 'Who is she then?'

'I don't know her name, that's the trouble,' I explain. 'That and other things.'

'Like?'

'She's in Year 10 for a start.'

'Year 10? Uh, uh!' Gabby's tone is like a buzzer, rejecting the possibility of this relationship. But then she says, 'Hang on a minute though. It depends when her birthday is. I mean, technically speaking, she may not be that much older than you. You're one of the oldest in your year, you're nearly fourteen already. She could still be fourteen too.'

I hadn't thought of it like that.

'She doesn't look much older than me,' I say eagerly. But then reality strikes. 'She's never going to look at a Year 9 boy though, is she? Everyone'll take the piss out of her . . . or call her stuff.'

'Not necessarily. Depends if she swims with the current or battles against the tide. Some people have an alternative outlook on life.'

I think of the girl with her purple hair, man's waistcoat and big, floppy shirt, her stripy socks and walking boots, her bowler hat. 'She's definitely alternative.'

'That's all right then.' Outside a car horn blares and Gabby leaps to her feet. 'Got to go.' Then she pauses at the door and turns to look at me. 'You know something, Fee? You're quite mature for your age. With your looks and confidence . . . you could have anyone.'

'Get lost!' I say and throw a pillow off the bed at her.

'I mean it,' she says, sidestepping it neatly. 'You're hot. Ask Angie.'

Sometimes I think that kid is haunting me, like a little ginger wraith that materializes out of nowhere and hangs around, spooking me with his presence. Everywhere I go, he's there. Not that I think he's deliberately seeking me out. Often he looks alarmed when he spots me, like *I'm* shadowing him. I find him lingering outside the art room one day and I jump out of my skin when I walk out of the door and nearly fall over him.

'What do you want?' I bark. He turns away and disappears up the stairs without a word, a frightened, ghostly little apparition with bright red hair.

'Who was that?' The girl with purple hair is behind me. She's been in the art room all lunchtime like me, not that she's paid me a blind bit of notice. Still, it was nice being in the same room as her.

'Some kid in Year 7. He's freaking me out,' I say, delighted she's decided to talk to me again.

'A Year 7 kid is freaking you out?' She laughs, showing all her pretty white teeth, and I laugh with her. 'Which one?'

'The ginger kid,' I say and her face changes big time. Her jaw drops open, her lip curls up and she gasps in derision.

'Uhh? Bit of a label that! The *ginger* kid.'

'You know what I mean.' I feel uncomfortable, wrong-footed. I didn't mean anything by it.

'There's more to someone than the colour of their hair, you know!' she says glowering at me from beneath her purple fringe.

'I know that,' I say helplessly. It's not like I was calling him names or anything. It was just a way of identifying him, I want to tell her, but it's too late, she's stomped off up the stairs.

At the end of the day I see her hanging round outside school as if she's waiting for someone. For a second I hope it's me but she catches my eye and turns away. I decide, what the hell, I'm going over anyway to try and explain to her what I meant. Then suddenly, there's an armlock round my neck.

'Hi, gorgeous! You going my way?'

Angie. What is she like? She's on a mission to improve my street-cred. It's working too. From the corner of my eye I notice Slug and Slick taking it all in. Angie has spotted them and is acting up for their benefit.

'What are we doing tonight, babes?' she croons, wide-eyed, then she slips her arm through mine and we walk down the drive together, trying not to laugh. I can feel scores of envious eyes boring into the back of my skull.

As we pass the basketball courts, arm in arm, a commotion is going on. A gang of kids are chucking someone's blazer around. They've tied it up in a ball and are lobbing it from one to the other, laughing fit to burst as some poor little sod dashes about frantically, trying to wrest it from them. Finally a lanky Year 8 kid

jumps up and slams it through the net.

'Goal!' they all yell and the scorer charges about the court victorious, roaring his head off, arms straight up in the air like some football hero, and everyone laughs. The blazer's owner picks up the makeshift ball and starts to disentangle the sleeves but it's snatched from his hands, then the lanky guy grabs him round the waist and makes as if he's going to bundle him into the net as well. The rest shriek with laughter and rush to the Year 8 kid's aid, grabbing the smaller kid's arms, legs, any bit of him they can get their hands on, and haul him over to the basketball post.

The kid kicks out, twisting and turning, his skinny ribs exposed as his shirt rides up high and his trousers threaten to fall down over his hips. He's desperate.

It's him again. The ging . . . the boy I keep noticing.

'OY!' yells Angie, opening the wire gate and bounding on to the court. 'Leave him alone, you little thugs!'

The kid is dropped to the ground and the others melt away, the ringleader trying to save face by giving Angie a mouthful of abuse, but she grabs hold of him and he soon changes his tune. I give the kid a hand up then pick the blazer off the ground and dust it down before handing it back to him. It's pretty grubby and one sleeve is hanging off.

Been there.

Done that.

Know exactly what it feels like.

The kid takes it from me. His face is snotty and smeared with tears.

'Thanks,' he sobs and runs off down the drive.

To my surprise I quite enjoy creating my collage. You can actually learn quite a bit about yourself, you know, when you are asked to focus on what's important to you.

First I draw the outline of my face, longish and oval-shaped, then I paint it in with a light olive-brown wash, the colour of my skin. Gabby says it's not fair, a complexion like mine is wasted on a boy, though I don't see it's much different from hers. When it's dry I sketch in two eyes and paint long, thick lashes around them (another waste according to Gabby). Then I carefully glue a small photo of my little brother, Henry, beaming happily at the camera, into one eye and a picture of an apple in the other. Get it? It looks bizarre but striking.

Next lesson I glue the end of an old sketching pencil on to my paper as my nose. Easy! Short and straight. Then I spend the rest of the time meticulously constructing a mouth in the shape of a hammock out of string, glueing it on to the paper, and drawing a tiny figure of me lying in it, sketching. It takes me forever.

By the end of the lesson most people have finished and are queuing up to put their work on the wall. Jacko was

right after all, it was a fun thing to do. He comes over to admire mine.

'Can I take it home to finish it off, sir?'

'Yes. But bring it in tomorrow. I want to get this display up for Open Evening. And I want yours to be the centrepiece.'

'You haven't seen mine yet, sir!' says Slug and everyone, including Jacko, laughs. But I don't think Slug's joking. He's been working on it non-stop. Jacko's avoided him, grateful that he's getting on with his work for once, but I've caught a glimpse of it and it's pretty impressive.

As the class disperses I stay behind during break, making sure the hammock is securely glued.

'Wicked!' says a voice and I look up to see HER gazing with delight at my picture of me. I'd been concentrating so hard I hadn't even noticed her come in. She's wearing the bowler hat.

'Love the hat! You got it then?'

'Yeah, thanks to you. Cost me a fiver. Bargain of the century. Teachers keep telling me to take it off.'

'Jacko won't mind.'

'Nah.' She bends over to examine the picture of Henry, her chin in her hand. I examine her. She's so close I can count the freckles on the side of her nose. Twelve. I wonder if she's got the same number on the other side? 'Who's the kid?' she asks.

'My brother.'

'Cute. I've got a kid brother too,' she remarks conversationally. 'He's the apple of my eye as well.'

I smile at her, pleased that she's got the allusion, thrilled to bits that she's talking to me again. 'What's his name?'

'Conor.'

'What's yours?'

'Violet.'

'Violet!' My eyes move involuntarily to her hair and she laughs.

'I know. It's a terrible name, isn't it? I got sick of being teased about it so I decided to dye my hair to match.'

'What's wrong with it?' I ask. 'I think it's a really pretty name. It suits you.'

'Thanks.' She's different today, rosier. Her cheeks look a bit flushed. I count the freckles on the other side of her nose. Twelve. Perfect.

'You know what kids are like. They'll always find something to tease you about,' she continues. 'That's what I tell my brother. He gets teased a lot.' She hesitates like she's about to say something important and I wait, but then she just adds, 'I don't really know what to do about it.'

'Tell your parents?'

She pulls a face. 'He won't let me. He's afraid they'll come up to school and make a fuss.'

'I still get the mickey taken out of me,' I confess. She's so easy to talk to today.

'I noticed. That first lesson. Ignore them, they're just jealous.'

'Thanks. I do.'

I smile at her and she goes a shade rosier, I don't know why.

'I didn't mean it,' I say. 'Calling that kid ginger, the other day. I didn't mean anything bad by it.'

'I know,' she says. 'I know that now.'

Suddenly she bites her lip, like she's a bit nervous, then she says in a rush, 'How does your girlfriend feel about it?'

'What?' What girlfriend? Feel about what? 'What do you mean?'

'Your little brother, you know . . . being the apple of your eye.' I stare at her in surprise, not understanding the question. 'Sorry,' she says abruptly. 'None of my business.'

Then she turns away and bolts for the door, her cheeks on fire.

'Are you OK?' I ask, but it's too late. She's gone.

What was all that about? What did I do to make her react like that? I mean, we were getting on so well, then suddenly she went all funny. I didn't know girls of that age still blushed. I thought you'd got past it by the time you were in Year 10.

And what's this with the girlfriend? First time she speaks to me she says, 'Everyone knows Felix.' In that case she knows I haven't got a girlfriend. Then the next time she sees me she blows me out. And now she's acting like she's flipping Cinderella or one of those Jane Austen heroines, running off in the middle of a conversation.

I think I'm changing my mind about girls. They're too complicated. Boys are much more straightforward. At least you always know where you are with them.

I still can't stop thinking about her though.

As soon as I get home from school that day I lay my self-portrait out on the kitchen table and get to work.

'*What* is that?' asks Freddie.

'It's me.'

'Why've you got Henry in your eye?'

'Because he's important to me.'

'I'm important to you. Put me in your other eye.'

'No.'

'MUM! It's not fair! Felix won't put me in his eye!'

'Felix!' says Mum automatically. 'Put Freddie in your . . . What are you doing?'

'Art homework.'

She comes over to inspect it and looks puzzled. 'Is that really art?'

'Yes, it's a collage.'

'Who is it meant to be?'

'Me.'

'Good grief.' She turns her head from side to side, examining it from different angles. 'Oh yes, I can see it now. How clever,' she adds unconvincingly, then, 'Make sure you finish it before your father comes home, Felix sweetheart. Only he won't call it art and he definitely won't think it's homework.'

I carry on, aided by Henry who is very into painting and sticking. He runs back and forth happily, rummaging through the recycling bins, finding me scraps of paper and packaging and discarded black wool from one, and eggshells, tea bags, and an assortment of vegetable peelings from the other to stick on to my picture. Thanks, Henry.

I take a set of coloured fine-line pens and start to sketch on the brow of my self-portrait, where the front of the brain would be if you could see it. Draw what is important to you, Jacko said. I don't even think about it, I just doodle what's in my head, which is the method I usually employ when I do my designs. A girl's face slowly emerges and I add detail: tiny freckles here, a row of studs there and spiky

hair which I carefully shade in purple. It looks like a large postage stamp stuck in the middle of my forehead.

'Pretty lady,' says Henry admiringly as he climbs up on to my lap to see.

'Very pretty,' I agree as I stare glumly at my picture.

Why don't I think before I act? I have just tattooed the face of the girl I'm obsessed with bang in the centre of my self-portrait. Which will be on display in the art room for everyone to see.

There is no way I've got time to start again.

'Hair?' suggests Henry.

Brilliant. I sift carefully through the stuff that Henry has collected, discarding the eggshells, tea bags and veggie peelings.

Then I cut the paper, string and wool into different lengths and glue them in thick strands on to the head of my collage. And by the time my father comes home, a rather strange-looking but highly effective fringe is in place, concealing from prying eyes the picture of the girl who has taken over my life, and my collage is safely back in my folder.

At home I start a new clothing collection. I do two a year, have done since I was about ten. My dream is to become a designer, creating new seasonal looks with my own label. Mostly I do women's clothes, though sometimes I'll experiment with men's clothes too. But women are more fun to design for, they love to dress up.

This time I have a very definite look in mind. It's kind of sexy tomboy, bordering on tough – lots of leather and denim, studs and chains, but with soft feminine touches that rescue it from grunge. So I mix studded leather jackets with floaty dresses, oversized dungarees with floral shirts, big heavy boots with figure-hugging mini-dresses, asymmetric torn denim jeans with soft clinging cardis.

All the models have short spiky hair in luminescent colours: bright yellow, shocking pink, petrol blue, purple. Mostly purple.

And their trademark look is, each one of them is wearing, clutching or waving . . . a bowler hat.

Autumn, by Felix.

'That is so cool,' says Gabby when I show it to her. She's always been a big fan of mine. 'I love the look. You should

show these to Mr Jackson, you know.'

'D'you reckon?' I've always been reluctant to show my designs to anyone outside the home. Or inside, come to that, except for Gabby or Mum. Dad and Freddie think it's weird that I sit around drawing girls in dresses all day. Goodness knows what Slug and his mates would have to say on the matter.

'These models, you know, they remind me of someone,' says Gabby, thumbing through my sketch book.

'Who?' I ask innocently.

'That girl in school.'

'Which one? There are loads of girls in school.'

'You know, the funky one. With the purple hair. She wears a bowler hat sometimes, I've seen her. I wonder what her name is?'

'Violet. She's in Year 10.'

'Oh my life!' Her eyes do that popping-out-on-strings thing again that she's so good at. 'It's her, isn't it? She's the one.'

I shrug my shoulders, trying to look nonchalant. 'Guess so. Is it that obvious?'

'Just a bit.' She grins at me sympathetically. 'She's really cool, Fee. Are you going to ask her out?'

'She's not interested.'

'How do you know? Talk to her.'

'I have! Sometimes she's really friendly and other times she just ignores me.'

'Maybe she's shy.'

'Does she look shy?'

'No.' Gabby looks thoughtful. 'I'll talk to Angie about it. She'll know what to do.'

'Back off, Gabby!'

'It'll be fine. Keep your hair on!'

'Gabby! I mean it! Don't interfere.'

'OK, OK, I won't,' she says soothingly. 'Trust me.'

Why is it that when someone says, 'Trust me', you know you can't?

Within five minutes I can hear her, on the phone to Angie.

At school everyone's getting ready for Open Evening. Jacko gives my collage pride of place in the Year 9 display as promised and proceeds to analyse it to the nth degree in front of everyone.

'This one I've put as our centrepiece because it's bright, bold and colourful, with clever use of materials,' he says, pointing at it with a ruler. 'Felix, explain to us the significance of the pencil for the nose.'

'I like drawing,' I say, wishing he'd shut up.

'Good. And the eyes? Tell us who this is a picture of.'

'My kid brother.'

'And the apple?'

I shrug. I'm good at shrugging. Jacko prattles on regardless.

'Felix's little brother is obviously the apple of his eye,' he explains to the class, like they're too thick to get it. 'Very clever. I like it.'

I don't. Not any more. He's ruining it, scrutinizing it in public like I'm on the syllabus. I can feel a wave of antipathy emanating from the class. Felix the creep.

'Well done, Felix. A good representation. But something tells me there is even more to you than you are telling us in this collage,' says Jacko.

'Oh there's definitely more to Felix,' says Slug unpleasantly and my skin tingles. I'm not scared of Slug any more, he's just a pain, but I know when there's trouble brewing.

He's mad, because he'd worked hard, I could tell he had. For once in his life Simon Lugg had tried, and his self-portrait was awesome, made up of pictures of fast cars and footballers cut from magazines he'd gone out and bought himself.

But all Jacko had noticed was the topless glamour models he'd placed coming out of the top of his head in thick felt-tip thought bubbles.

And all he'd said was, 'Bin it!'

'It's not fair!' growled Slug but he did as he was told and stuffed it in the bin. I actually felt sorry for him. Those thought bubbles were funny! Anyway, you can't ask someone to create a picture of themselves from the things that matter to them and then object to what they put in. Everyone knows that's all Slug thinks about: footie, fast cars and getting laid.

Now he's really pissed off. And when Slug is in this kind of mood, you'd better watch out. Jacko hasn't noticed, he's too busy burbling on about my collage, which now looks childish and immature to me.

Teachers have got a lot to answer for. I mean, I would normally rate Jacko higher than most, but I know why he won't put Slug's work on display for Open Evening. He's scared he'll get flak from parents like mine. Like my dad anyway. Teachers get bullied too.

It's a shame because Slug's collage may not be very subtle but it's good. Jacko needs to stop trying to get inside my head and notice him instead. Then maybe he'd see beyond the bluster and bravado and big 'I Am' and see the real Simon Lugg who'd finally shown a spark of interest and made a real effort for once.

Who'd have thought I would ever find myself championing Simon Lugg? But from the look on his face I know I'm in trouble. When someone like me is seen as being treated as special it doesn't do them any favours. Teacher's pet and all that.

It just makes the other kids mad.

When everyone's gone I nick Slug's collage from the bin and smooth it out.

It's too good to be binned.

I slide it into my folder.

Outside the art room, Slug is gagging for trouble. He'd probably like to smash my face in for stealing his thunder but that's not his way. I've come to realize over the years he's actually not that brave, but he conceals his cowardice well behind a sneering armoury of gobbiness.

'Watch out, everyone!' he yells as I walk out, trip over his outstretched leg and sprawl headlong into a load of kids walking the other way. 'Gay boy wants a cuddle!'

Not that again. This is the first time he's used the gay boy offensive since the time he saw Angie and me together on the common. I thought our snogging session had laid that particular taunt to rest, but obviously not. Homophobia features highly in his mass of insecurities. I draw myself up to my full height and turn to face him. I'm taller than him now. For a fleeting second panic etches itself on his face, then he laughs and saunters off down the corridor, his henchmen in tow.

I watch as he shoulders Slick into a couple of girls then stops to chat them up. Very subtle. Then my eyes narrow.

Just past him, near the end of the corridor, I can see two girls talking together intensely. One of them is Violet. The other one is Angie. My stomach shrivels up into a

tiny knot of embarrassment as my sister's words come back to me.

'I'll talk to Angie about it. She'll know what to do.'

I knew she'd interfere!

What is Angie saying to her?

The next second two things happen at once.

The girls Slug and Slick are trying to chat up blow them out big time. One of them, with a look of disdain, pushes Slug away, straight into a random passing kid who is knocked flying. Slug, already in a dangerous mood and with his ego severely dented, kicks out at the kid's bag as it falls to the floor and at the same time, Violet turns on her heel away from Angie, her face livid, and sees what he's doing.

Slug disappears from sight, his laughter braying back like a phantom donkey as he tries to redeem some face from the situation. Violet and I meet mid-corridor and haul the kid to his knees.

It's him again. The ginger kid. I don't believe it. This has got to be the unluckiest kid on the planet.

'You OK?' I ask as he dusts himself down. He nods blindly, looking more than a little bemused. Violet curses loudly as she fusses over him.

'That Slug should be locked up!' she spits. 'I'm going to kill him!'

'To be fair, I don't think he meant to do it,' I say magnanimously. Then I wish I'd kept my mouth shut as she turns on me.

'He kicked his bag!' she yells. 'I saw him!'

'Yeah. But I don't think he meant to knock him over.'

Why am I sticking up for Slug of all people?

She looks at me as if I've got a screw loose. 'He's done it before!' she shouts. 'It's not the first time! They're always picking on him.'

'I know,' I say helplessly.

'Come on, Conor,' she says and grabs his bag, stuffing everything back into it. 'I've had enough of this. We're going to report it.'

'No!' he says, his eyes wide with fear.

'Yes!' she says and hauls him off. The kid looks back at me for help but there's nothing I can do.

Conor.

He's her kid brother. The apple of her eye.

Suddenly she stops and looks back at me too.

'And by the way!' she says scornfully. 'There was absolutely no need to get your girlfriend to warn me off, lover boy. I wouldn't touch you with a bargepole if you were the last person on the planet.'

I slope off to the canteen, my head spinning with the injustices of life. It seems like I've blown it big time with Violet and none of it is my fault.

Angie? My girlfriend?

No way.

So what is she doing, 'warning Violet off'?

And, just as crazy, how did I end up defending Slug and his bullying ways?

As luck would have it, as soon as I enter the canteen I come face to face with him, making his noisy way to a table, his tray piled high. The sight of his jeering face is enough to send me over the edge from quietly fuming to mad as hell. How dare he and Angie between them muck things up between Violet and me!

Before I know what I'm doing, I'm giving it to him straight, right there in the middle of the canteen, in front of everyone.

'Why don't you pick on someone your own size?' I challenge, barring his way.

'Eh?' He looks confused. I've got him at a disadvantage, he hasn't a clue what I'm on about. The room falls silent.

'You wanna kick someone's bag around, kick mine,' I

snarl. 'But leave little Year 7 kids alone.'

A cheer goes up. As understanding dawns, Slug looks angry but he's stuck with a heavy tray-load of carbohydrates in his fists. All he can do is swear a lot and promise me in no uncertain terms what he's going to do to me when his hands are free. The next minute a teacher wades in to sort us out, directing me to the lunch queue and Slug to a table. The show is over.

I take a deep breath, thank my lucky stars we didn't come to blows, and treat myself to some cheese and pickle sandwiches.

'Felix! Over here!'

Angie is waving at me from the corner of the canteen. OK. No time like the present, might as well have words with her too. I make my way over to her, noting, too late, as I place my sandwiches on the table, that Slug is sitting with his mates on the table behind. Tough!

'What have you been saying to Violet?' I ask as I sit down.

'Ah!' she says and looks a bit embarrassed.

I never did get the answer.

That's the last thing I remember.

Apparently my chair was whipped away from under me, one of the oldest tricks in the book. By Slug, needless to say.

And I'm knocked out stone cold as soon as my head lands with a sickening crack on the floor.

Slug was immediately suspended and I was whisked off to hospital in an ambulance. I was all right, I'd come round by then, but they still said I had to go and be properly checked out in case I had concussion.

I didn't mind. I got to miss double science. By the time my dad arrived they said I was OK to go home.

'Strong lad you've got there,' says the nurse. 'He's had a nasty whack on the head but no real damage done.'

'Thick skull,' says Dad, playing it down, but managing to look dead proud of me at the same time.

When he found out how it happened, he was prouder of me still. Gabby was full of it when she got home. The story had got round school, embellished somewhat, how I'd stood up to Slug and his gastropods in the canteen to save a Year 7 kid and been beaten up for my trouble. I am a hero apparently.

'It wasn't like that,' I say but nobody's listening.

Mr Roberts the head teacher comes round later to see how I am and assures Mum and Dad in a very loud, serious voice that 'THE SCHOOL TAKES A VERY FIRM STAND INDEED ON BULLYING' and it was 'VERY MUCH ON HIS AGENDA' but he acknowledges,

'THERE IS STILL MORE TO DO.' He drones on so much about 'CAMPAIGNS' and 'INITIATIVES' and 'MENTORING' and 'ADDRESSING ISSUES' it makes my head ache. When I mention this after he's finally gone, Mum makes me go to bed.

I lie there, unable to sleep. I get texts from Rhys and Logan, Deepak and Sean and loads of girls, asking how I am and saying that Slug got what was coming to him. I don't know though. I'm not sure he did. I actually feel a bit sorry for him. All he did was pull my chair away from under me, the sort of thing that kids do to each other every day. I mean, I know it's stupid, but it's not exactly a hanging offence, is it?

The house is quiet. Freddie and Henry have gone to bed, Gabby's out, Dad's watching telly in the lounge. Mum's online as usual.

My phone bleeps. Again. So this is what it feels like to be popular. It's from Angie.

I open the message and nearly have a heart attack.

I stare at the text in bewilderment.

Are you good in bed?

That's what it says. I kid you not.

That is sick!

Why is Angie coming on to me? She's like my own sister. My big sister! I've known her since I was eight and she was eleven!

She's in the Sixth Form for goodness sake!

I'm in Year 9.

She can't fancy me!

She does. She must.

It's obvious. Like, we've always got on. And she's always said I'm gorgeous. I never thought anything about it. I think she's gorgeous too. But not in *that* way.

Think about the events of the past few weeks though. What about that snog? I mean, I thought she was just having a laugh, giving me a bit of a boost in front of Slug and that lot. But, maybe that was just an excuse. It did go on a bit.

My blood chills as I remember something else.

Gabby said Angie thought I was hot! And there's me thinking she was just being kind.

Plus, today Violet told me that Angie had warned her off. I'd seen her with my own eyes. She'd said she was *my girlfriend*.

And now this!

I read the text again.

And again.

Are you good in bed?

This is cyberbullying! It's worse than Slug pulling a stupid chair from under me! I close the text hurriedly and snap my phone shut.

Immediately it rings and I snatch it back up.

My eyes widen.

It's her again.

It's Angie.

I switch my phone off and pull the duvet up over my head.

Mum lets me sleep in the next morning so I miss school.

'It won't hurt for once,' she says when I finally surface. Suits me! 'Anyway, it's Open Evening tonight. And the Head has asked specifically to meet with us.'

I hang out with Henry all day, watching CBeebies, snacking on Coco Pops, playing with dinosaurs. When he's woken up from his afternoon sleep (I must confess I have a bit of a nap too), we raid the bag of old clothes Mum's put ready for the charity shop and play dressing up, which was always my favourite game when I was a kid. Gabby used to dress me up as the Wicked Queen, which was probably about the time Dad started to get a bit anxious about what sort of son he'd produced.

I've got news for you, Dad. Your youngest son loves dressing up in women's clothes too!

By the time the others come home I must admit I'm pleased to see them. Henry is ace but his vocabulary only stretches to about two hundred words so conversation can become a bit repetitive. Now I see why Mum spends so much time blogging, no offence, Henry.

'Why's your phone switched off?' asks Gabby as we're

leaving for Open Evening. 'Angie's been trying to get hold of you all day.'

My head jerks up in alarm. 'Has she? What for?'

She shrugs. 'She wants to know if you're OK. You know how much she loves you.'

I'm beginning to. I switch on my phone. Five missed phone calls and a million missed messages, all from Angie. I go to open them but Mum snatches the phone from my hand and stuffs it in her bag.

'Give that thing to me or we'll be late. You'll see her in a minute.'

'I don't want to see her!' I mumble.

Gabby and Mum raise their eyebrows at each other. 'Moo-dy!' says Gabby and they both laugh.

Women!

At school I slip into the art room before I catch up with the others. Then we trail round together as a family, listening to teachers waxing lyrical about Gabby's musical prowess, Gabby's gift for languages, Gabby's love of literature. No wonder the Gemstones hated her.

I can see why Slug gets so pissed off with me now.

In the art room, there are masses of people standing round our display of collages. They're causing quite a stir, especially the one in the middle. Dad's face is a picture when he studies it.

'Very avant-garde!' he says disapprovingly. 'I don't call that art!'

Mum smirks at me and steers him away to the safety of the maths block. I hang back, hoping I can lose them.

'Hi. This must be Henry?'

Violet is beside me, bending down to talk to my little brother who is hanging on to my leg. I gaze at the top of her head in surprise. She is so unpredictable. I never know what to expect from this girl. She wasn't this friendly the last time I saw her!

'Yeah, this is Henry. That's Freddie over there.' Freddie scowls at her as he continues peeling blu-tack off the wall, bored out of his skull, and she giggles and stands up.

'I want to thank you,' she says, looking me straight in the eye. Her cheeks are pink and she's prettier than ever.

'What for?'

'Sticking up for Conor. I heard about what you did in the canteen.'

It's my turn to turn pink.

'How's your head?'

'Fine.'

'I owe you an apology too . . .'

'FELIX!!!'

I look up and groan. Angie is bearing down on me.

'I've been trying to get hold of you all day! Did you get my text?'

'Not now, Angie!'

'No listen! That text I sent you last night. It was a mistake.'

Some mistake.

'I rang you straight away to explain but you didn't answer. I realized immediately what I'd done!' Her face is

full of concern. 'I didn't mean it!'

'Forget it!' I mumble, wishing she'd shut up and go away.

She stares at me dismayed. 'You haven't listened to the messages I left you or read my texts, have you?'

'No.'

It's her turn to groan. 'Let me explain . . .'

'It doesn't matter,' I say and turn away but she grabs me by the arm. 'No, listen! Predictive text, Felix. Think about it.'

I stare at her blankly.

'You've got it all wrong,' she says earnestly. 'That text . . . Look, write the same message yourself.'

'What?'

'Do it! When you come to "good", press "star". It will all make sense.' She smiles at us both. Then she disappears out of the room, leaving Violet and me staring at each other, totally bewildered.

'What was all that about?' asks Violet.

'Don't ask me,' I say. 'But I promise you one thing. She is NOT my girlfriend.'

'Really?' Violet looks different. Sort of shy and . . . hopeful.

I take a deep breath. 'There is only one girl I want to go out with.'

Her face positively glows. 'Who would that be then?'

Henry bored with life at hip level, starts tugging on my leg. 'Up, Fee! Up!' he orders.

I pull him up into my arms. Spotting my collage on

the wall he shrieks with delight and stretches out his arms towards it.

'Mine!' he says and before I can stop him he tugs with both hands at the fringe he so lovingly helped me to assemble. It comes off to reveal, tattooed on my brain, a picture of a girl with purple hair.

I turn to Violet.

'That one,' I say.

Much later that night, when everyone else is asleep in bed, I remember Angie and steal downstairs to get my phone from Mum's bag. I ignore her subsequent messages and go straight to the original text.

There it is.

Are you good in bed?

I still can't believe she'd send me a text like that.

What was it she'd told me to do?

'Write the same message yourself,' she'd said. 'When you come to "good" press "star".'

I do as she says, then as an alternative word flashes up I get it at last and start shaking with silent laughter.

The text reads:

Are you home in bed?

I flash through the rest of her messages. Poor Angie. She was mortified. She was only checking up if I was home from hospital. She'd realized her mistake as soon as she'd pressed 'send'. Then she'd left endless messages, explaining what had actually happened. She kept running out of message space and had to keep ringing me to give me the full story.

It turns out she hadn't been warning Violet off at all.

Egged on by Gabby, she'd been trying to get us together.

'Are you interested in Felix?' she'd asked, when she stopped her in the corridor. And Violet, thinking that Angie was going out with me, because she'd seen us together, hadn't she, on the common, walking out of school, our arms wrapped round each other, had denied it flatly.

Even though she liked me. A lot.

Anyway, it's all straightened out now. As from this evening, thanks to, or maybe in spite of, Gabby and Angie and Henry and Conor and even Slug, in a way, we're officially an item. And neither of us gives a stuff about her being in Year 10 and me in Year 9.

After all, most people assumed I was going out with a Year 12 girl anyway!

Oh, and I know how cheesy this sounds, but we're setting up a peer mentoring programme at our school too, to tackle bullying. Gabby, Angie, Violet, Conor and me. Mr Roberts asked us tonight if I knew of any other kids who might want to join us who may have had experience of bullying.

'Yeah,' I said. 'Simon Lugg.'

He thought I was joking at first but I wasn't.

Like I said to him, we need people like Slug to join us, and teachers and parents too. Then maybe we'd all learn to accept each other a bit more, stop labelling each other. We're all guilty of it, me included.

I mean, I object to the names he calls me.

Poofter, gay boy, fairy, geek . . .

Not very nice, are they? But then I've got to be honest, I do it as well. What do I call Slug?

Thicko, psycho, headbanger, moron . . .

They're just as bad.

Maybe it's time we cut the labels off.

I've made a start.

He's already worked out it was me that stuck his collage back up on the wall tonight for Open Evening.

In pride of place.

Where it deserved to be.

FLIP OVER FOR ANOTHER EXCITING READ . . .

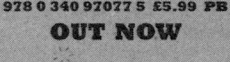